D0955996

Praise for *Sarajevo Blues*

"Semezdin Memedinović charts the collapse of a world with heartbreaking clarity and precision . . . Conveys the same clear-eyed passion for the truth that one finds in the young Hemingway, the Hemingway of our time."
—PAUL AUSTER, author of *4 3 2 1* and *The Brooklyn Follies*

"*Sarajevo Blues* is widely considered here to be the best piece of writing to emerge from the besieged capital since Bosnia's war erupted in April 1992."　　　　　—*The Washington Post*

"Mr. Mehmedinović left his native Bosnia in 1996, but his record of the horrifying events he observed there is vividly immediate. In short pieces of prose and poetry the author recaptures the stoicism created by constant danger and the incongruous survival of pre-war habits . . . The mundane and the terrible merged in Sarajevo. Mr. Mehmedinović takes the reader there."　　　　—PHOEBE LOU ADAMS, *The Atlantic*

"[The] ability to masterfully delineate even the simplest moments but somehow remain tactfully indifferent is Mehmedinović's most invaluable attribute . . . It is as if you are being 'pulled' into this world, where the vigor of his words and the sharpness of his eye lead the way . . . A memorable literary achievement."　　　　　　　　　　—*Library Journal*

MY HEART

MY HEART

A Novel

✦

Semezdin Mehmedinović

TRANSLATED FROM THE BOSNIAN BY
CELIA HAWKESWORTH

✦

WITH AN INTRODUCTION BY
ALEKSANDAR HEMON

CATAPULT  NEW YORK

Copyright © 2017 by Semezdin Mehmedinović and Fraktura.
All rights are represented by Fraktura, Croatia.
English translation copyright © 2021 by Celia Hawkesworth
Introduction copyright © 2021 by Aleksandar Hemon

ISBN: 978-1-646220-07-6

Jacket design by Dana Li
Book design by Wah-Ming Chang

Library of Congress Control Number: 2020942074

Printed in the United States of America

1 3 5 7 9 10 8 6 4 2

INTRODUCTION

by Aleksandar Hemon

Some years ago, I visited Semezdin Mehmedinović and his family in their Virginia suburb. One evening, we decided to play some basketball on a nearby court. I don't remember why or how exactly, but we ended up playing with a deflated ball in complete darkness. We couldn't see the basket, the ball didn't bounce, we didn't have teams or keep score. It was the greatest basketball game I've ever played in my life, because I remember myself as being totally present in it. It is precisely this sense of total presence that I desire from literature, and that Semezdin Mehmedinović never fails to generate.

I have long felt a kinship with Mehmedinović's work, as we share a native language, a love for the city of Sarajevo, and a whole world of literary influences, acquaintances, and references. I consider him to be my favorite living writer in our native language—Bosnian—or, for that matter, in any other language. His book *Sarajevo Blues*, a collection of poems and prose fragments written during the siege of Sarajevo, is immensely important to me and arguably the greatest book to have emerged from the experience of the Bosnian war.

Yet I am still astonished by the impact and the beauty of *My Heart*, Mehmedinović's most recent book published in English. I had read in Bosnian each of the three parts that constitute the book, and when I read it again in Celia Hawkesworth's wonderful translation, I marveled once more at the precision of his observations, his sensitivity to detail, and his incredible ability to be present in the world while observing it.

Each of the three parts of the book—"Me'med," "Red Bandana," and "Snowflake"—deals, in a slightly different way, with the bread and butter of art and literature: love and death, and the suddenly enhanced presence of each in Mehmedinović's life. Each piece is structured as a journey—the writer is unmoored from the harbor of home—that replicates the situation of displacement, internal and external, caused by the war. And on each journey, Mehmedinović generates endless discoveries of what was once familiar and is now strange again, because that is the effect of time and the presence of death, as inseparable as Siamese twins with a shared heart, on a thinking writer.

Mehmedinović's language is simple, but only because his vision is clear; his sentences are determined and peaceful, as though conditioned by an inner calm rooted in his indelible wandering worldliness—there is a stable center of love inside him, necessary in a world that is inherently unstable. He is the kind of writer who sees just as clearly and calmly under siege as when driving in Virginia. His literature is equally at home, or equally not at home, in any and all places.

Though *My Heart* is autobiographical in the sense that the person in the book is the person who wrote it, nothing about it is memoiristic or confessional, and certainly never indulgent or self-centered. Experience is refracted in the world, just as the world is refracted in the experience, while the writing is not descriptive but defamiliarizingly reflective and transformative. Mehmedinović generates knowledge—about love, life, death, family, exile, displacement, past, memory—that is not available otherwise, but his need to do so is both personal (if I don't remember, who will?) and ethical (if I don't remember, no one will). "We spend a lot of time remembering the past," he writes in "Snowflake," "that's how we check how much of everything we've forgotten."

MY HEART

.

ME'MED

Today, it seems, was the day I was meant to die.

I was getting ready for work, taking a shower, when I felt a dull, metallic pain in my chest and throat, and the taste of cement on my tongue. I stepped out of the shower feeling indescribably tired and wrapped my wet body in a bathrobe. Sanja was just about to leave the apartment to go to work, but then she caught sight of me through the open bathroom door. I told her I wasn't feeling well, I was going back to bed for a bit, this *weariness* would soon pass, and she shouldn't hesitate to go.

She stayed. Wet, my hair dripping, wrapped in the bathrobe, I stretched out on the bed. And I felt increasingly bad. She brought me cold tea, which didn't help, and then, having no choice, she called 911. After that, she stared out at the street impatiently, looking for the ambulance. I didn't have the energy to turn onto my other side so as to watch her by the window. I looked at the sofa where she had been sitting. I felt suddenly uneasy because she wasn't where she had just been. Then I looked at the photograph on the wall above the sofa:

Lhasa. Early morning. A young Buddhist priest had come out through a high wooden door in the wall of a stone building, and was now walking down a narrow cobbled lane, with a wisp of morning mist in front of him. A small white cloud. Like a ghost that the priest in his red robe was following. I let my gaze follow the white cloud above the cobblestones in Tibet.

Behind me, Sanja said: "Here they are." Then she came back into my field of vision. She opened the door and looked down the corridor, anxiously, occasionally glancing toward me. And then our room was filled with strangers from the emergency services, settling themselves briskly around me on the sofa. I had never experienced such an aggressive assault on my privacy. Quite uninhibited and sure of themselves, they glanced around the room they had come to, glanced at me, admired the floral pattern of the bedspread I was lying on, strangers in my room.

A girl in a blue uniform had just opened my bathrobe, so that I lay before them naked, and asked: "How old are you, sir?"

"Fifty."

After the initial shock, there was calm.

I looked at everything around me without emotion, and so—without fear. And now that it's over, I remember the event as though I had seen it from a distance, as though my mind had become separate from my body and had observed what was going on almost with indifference.

The shock didn't come when the girl in the blue uniform said: "Sir, you're having a heart attack!"

That's when I felt calm. Because my mind had overcome my emotions. In films, when people describe a critical moment such as this, the picture is often left without sound, and sometimes it's even in slow motion. That's a technical evocation of the mind at work.

The mind behaves like a cold camera lens.

In this case the shock had come at the moment when the ambulance arrived, especially when a bunch of strangers filled my room. This was something that happened to other people, not to me, and it was something I recoiled from, of which I had a natural fear. And here my fear of illness was expressed as fear of doctors and hospitals. I never went to hospitals even as a visitor.

And now the girl in the blue uniform leaned over me on my sofa, and said: "You're having a heart attack!"

My first thought: She's wrong, this isn't my heart. Then I thought: I know this girl from somewhere. I tried to remember where from, but now there were a lot of human hands above me, attaching me to wires, turning me to the left, then to the right, disturbing my train of thought: I couldn't remember where I had seen the girl before. Through her blue blouse, I saw the outline of her breasts, but didn't register that as in any way sexual. She was looking at me anxiously, as though accusing me of something.

And one other optical impression: The bodies of all those people around me were unnaturally large, while my body had shrunk. What was it I was feeling? Weariness. Weariness from the pressure in my chest, which was making me breathless, which had become the same as weariness with life. And I thought: So, is that it? So, is this death? At that moment, in fact, I began to see everything not just as a participant but also as an outside observer. And I thought: It's good, just let it all pass, I'm tired, I want to close my eyes and not remember. I want it all to stop.

All I had lived through up to now was already too much.

On the way to the hospital, lying in the ambulance, my knee crushed by the weight of an oxygen canister, I watched the passing clouds, the green traffic signals that I had noticed up until then only as a driver. Through the back door of the ambulance, after we slowed down for something, I saw a sign on the façade of a brick building with the inscription LIBERATION BOOKS. I had only seen that inscription before on a photograph of Harun's. And later, when I went with him to look at the books there, we weren't able to find the shop. He remembered it as being somewhere near the junction of King and Henry Streets. There was no information about the bookshop on the internet. I had searched in vain for it the previous week as well, and now I was looking at the girl in the blue uniform leaning over me to fix my headrest and thinking how ridiculous it would be to ask: "What's the name of this street?"

As though I'd ever have a chance to find LIBERATION BOOKS! But books have a certain power over us nevertheless. If this weren't the case, during my dramatic ride to the hospital, I wouldn't have noticed the inscription LIBERATION BOOKS. Or was my mind turning to anything else, just to forget the pain in my chest? The young man sitting by my feet kept shifting the heavy metal canister that was lying on my legs. He shifted it so that the cold metal lay uncomfortably against the bone of my knee, and for a while that became the dominant pain in my body. This made me silently furious with the young man, who was, perhaps, scraping the oxygen canister against my knees on purpose, intending to deflect my mind away from my heart to a different problem.

Then I turned my attention to the tops of the trees lining the street, the leaves were reddish brown, before they fell. In the autumn, the leaves here take on such dazzling, sunny colors that even on a cloudy day one has the impression of a surplus of light. Was it a sunny morning? Or did the colors in the treetops give me an illusion of sun? I had always been disturbed by the thought of dying in a landscape where deciduous trees grew. There was something unconvincing, something *obvious* about it.

It was somehow indecent to die in the autumn.

It was kitsch to die in the autumn, along with everything else. With the leaves.

The ambulance stopped in front of the hospital. In the parking lot, the first image I saw from my horizontal position was this: walking between the cars toward the hospital building was a girl in the red hockey shirt of the Washington Capitals. She was looking upward, toward a window, or at a cloud.

I had only ever been in this parking lot once before, when the wife of the poet F. was giving birth to their little daughter. I remember that he had bought a new Toyota Camry that day, and asked me: "Would you like to drive it?" "Sure." And I drove once around the parking lot. That was ten years ago. I can still remember the smell of the new car.

My oxygen mask began to mist up in the icy November air.

In the hospital entrance, I was met by a choir of smiling medical personnel. On my right, a nurse struggled to find a vein in my arm to take blood. On my left, two girls in green coats were gazing and marveling at the design of the bedspread I was wrapped in. At the same time, I caught sight of Sanja at the end of the corridor, a man (a doctor?) had just come up to her with some papers in his hand, she listened carefully to what he said and then began to cry.

The man was now leaning over me. He felt my pulse with cold fingers, and asked: "How old are you?"

"Fifty."

✦

I want to go back to my apartment for a moment.

What is the answer to the question "Who am I while strangers are examining my naked body in my own room?" And among them is that girl, whom I know from somewhere. What fills me with unease, and muffled shame, is not the proximity of death, but the realization that my body, at this moment, is an object conveying nothing. My corporality is asexual.

What is more, the ease with which these strangers shift my body through space creates an impression of my own weightlessness. I am what is left of me, my mortal remains, as I lie in my bathrobe, under which I am naked.

All I know about the body I know as a poet, and that is pretty selective, limited to those characteristics in which the body displays its advantages and its strength, and not its weaknesses and shortcomings.

About the diseases of the body, I actually know nothing.

The mind draws logical conclusions on the basis of data accessible to it, and when the attack happened, while I was standing under the shower in the bathroom, I immediately connected the pain in my throat and metallic taste in my mouth with an article I had read in *Vanity Fair*. It was an account of an attack experienced by the author (Christopher Hitchens, who was later diagnosed with cancer), and in that description he says he felt pain in his chest and neck, and something like "the slow drying of cement" in his chest. (I'm quoting this from memory, but I think those were the words he used to describe his state, which was what I was now experiencing.) And when I came out of the shower and the pain in my chest got worse, I was convinced that I had cancer.

Later, the emergency services arrived, and the girl (a doctor in a blue uniform) leaned over me and said: "Sir, you are having a heart attack!"

And my first thought had been: No, dear. This can't be my heart. My mind was so firmly convinced that my symptoms were like those in the description of Hitchens's attack that I favored the account from his article over the official diagnosis. In any case, at one moment I thought: This is comical! I'm dying thinking about Christopher Hitchens!

It was comical: my reality, at such a crucial moment, was being explained by a columnist in *Vanity Fair*, who didn't know I existed and so couldn't know, either, that I was, perhaps, right now ceasing to exist.

"How old are you?"

"Fifty."

This is a dialogue that has kept being repeated today.

The number of years I had lived represented important information for the doctors. I had the feeling that, in this way, for the first time—in this long life—my time was being accurately measured. This meant that today all my illusions of youth vanished. We rationalize our experience of time, but beyond the givens of the calendar, we are not conscious of it. Because "in spirit" we stay the same. "In spirit" I was the same person I had been in my twenties. That's how it is, probably, with everyone, it's a characteristic of our species. That's how we protect ourselves from death. Western cultures see man in his asymmetry and disharmony, so they separate him into a body that ages and a soul that doesn't age. Apart, presumably, from Dostoevsky.

Reduced to a body, lying on the operating table, I communicated the whole time with my eyes and through a meager exchange of words with various people who were working on my revival. This was a surprising number of people, those who prepared for the operation and those who participated in it. They all struck up conversations with the dying person, and my impression was that the body (i.e., me) did not offer much information, even on the operating table. Apart from my unpronounceable name, the only piece of information about me was this bedspread with the floral pattern à la Paul Gauguin, in which I was wrapped when I came here, everyone commented on it, interested in the cultural origin of the drawing on canvas, presumably convinced that the bedspread had the same geographical origin as myself.

At one point the surgeon who was operating on me, not

knowing how to negotiate my complicated name, brought his face close to mine and explained, slightly alarmed, that he would have to communicate with me in the course of the operation and for that communication he would need a name to call me by. He said: "I'll call you Me'med. Is that okay?"

As for the bedspread, I don't know exactly where it came from, other than that it was some South American country. Perhaps from the same country as one of the hospital staff who took such an interest in it. In any case, these people treated my origin with great sensitivity, although they didn't ask, nor, I presume, did they know where I came from. From my accent they knew only that I was foreign.

Does this mean that we all suffer from a kind of anxiety about dying in a distant, foreign country that is not our own, a world where we are not at home?

This is the first time I see inside my body: on the left of the operating table is a screen on which is projected an image of my cardiac arteries. What I see reminds me of a branching plant. One very thin, almost transparent twig had begun to grow and lengthen. Behind that *growth* was an unknown, delicate procedure that the doctor applied to my blocked artery, so as to break through the blockage and enable the normal flow of blood. Instantly I felt indescribable relief. The same procedure was applied to the other artery: I watched as the branch grew before my eyes.

And that was it. The pain in my throat and pressure in my chest disappeared. The moment of liberated breathing was so refreshing that all trace of tiredness left my body. This made me want to straighten up, to get off the operating table and walk.

Full of oxygen.

The theater unexpectedly emptied, for a short time I was alone, and I heard a buzzing but didn't know what was making the sound. A machine? Or a fly in the air?

Then the room filled up with human voices again. None of them took any notice of me. They were discussing the previous night's episode of the television series *Big Bang Theory*.

And they were laughing.

An African American girl leaned over me and asked: "Would you like me to bring some water?"

I said: "Yes, please."

Someone else in the room was describing how he had spent half an hour that morning stuck in an elevator. The person responsible for the elevator had finally appeared, and when he had been freed, he felt, he said, "like a Chilean miner who had just been brought out of the earth into the sun."

I drank water out of a plastic cup. And I couldn't remember when I was last so aware of the taste of ordinary, sweet water.

From the operating theater, lying on a narrow stretcher, I was taken by elevator to the ward. I was accompanied by two young people in hospital coats; they weren't in a hurry to go anywhere, they were talking, laughing, and easily forgot my presence. They could have been lovers. In their company, I felt my primary characteristics returning to my body. When we entered the elevator, it turned out that my height in a horizontal position was such that they had trouble fitting me into the moving box of the elevator. And when the doors closed, I could feel them rubbing against my feet as we moved.

All the people I meet today disappear. They vanish before I have a chance to say goodbye. Those two young lovers who had been chirruping and laughing in the elevator as they took me from the lower to the upper floors, they, too, left without my noticing the moment of their departure.

In my ward, a new nurse settled me in the bed and said: "Lovely bedspread."

I said I had brought it from home. Then she explained that I could by all means keep it here as well; maybe she believed I had a childish emotional attachment to that rug.

Then I called Sanja, who had gotten lost somewhere in the depressing architecture of the hospital corridors.

If a line is drawn under Tuesday, 2 November 2010, this is what happened to me:

As I was getting ready to go to work, I had a heart attack.

I was in the shower when I felt a dull, metallic pressure

in my chest and throat, and when, soon afterward, the ambulance arrived, the girl who examined me said, bluntly and without beating about the bush: "You're having a heart attack." Under an oxygen mask, I watched Sanja on the sofa opposite the bed where I was lying surrounded by strangers. Her face was contorted with fear. They hurried to take me away, wrapped in the cover on which I was lying, they took me to hospital, and then I had an operation. And after they had installed stents in my blocked arteries, I was settled into a hospital ward. It all took a little more than three hours, but during that time my world, and me in it, were fundamentally altered.

After the operation, the doctor looked for Sanja, but she wasn't in the waiting room. When they'd put me into the ward, I called her on her cell phone. She answered, she was on her way. She came into the room, pale, her face swollen with crying. That face expressed the uncontrolled joy and absolute sorrow that had entirely overwhelmed her. Something in her was broken. She had an irresistible urge to hug me but didn't dare for fear that she might hurt me. I asked her to sit on the bed, beside me.

"Where were you?"

"Outside the hospital."

"It's cold outside, and you're dressed like *that* . . ." I'd only just noticed that—in her haste—she had simply put a little sweater on over her T-shirt.

"I didn't dare wait."

"What do you mean?"

"I was afraid the doctor was going to come and tell me . . ."

"Tell you what?"

"That you'd died."

"It hadn't quite come to that."

"When I was giving them permission to operate, they asked if I wanted them to fetch a priest."

"What did you say?"

"I said there was no need for that, and that you weren't going to die."

"You didn't tell them that a priest couldn't reconcile me to God . . ."

"No."

"You should have!" I said, joking.

She pretended to be cross (people were dying here and he was having a laugh!), then she slapped my chest gently with her open hand, then at the same instant remembered my heart and shuddered, she could have hurt me oh oh oh she waved her hands in the air over me ohohohooo. Then we laughed.

I remember the rest of the day quite clearly as well.

When I was left alone in the ward, this is what I thought about:

Of course I had been thinking and all these years developing my attitude toward my own death, but I didn't expect it could come as a consequence of my heart stopping. All my other organs could stop functioning, but the heart was out of the question, it was there, I thought, to beat for me, just as long as I needed it.

I called Harun. He was now in St. Louis. At the airport.

"How long is it till your flight?"

"Six hours."

At midnight on 31 January 1996, on our way from Zagreb to Phoenix, Arizona, on our immigrant journey to America, we had been at the St. Louis airport.

We were changing planes.

I remember rows of gray leather seats in the waiting room, and midnight travelers with Stetsons. In those days there were ashtrays on high stands beside the seats, and the stale air reeked of Jack Daniel's. There wouldn't be any ashtrays there anymore. And now, as I chatted to Harun, I remembered a photograph from that journey. It was of him asleep, his head resting on his arms on a table in the airport café. He was thirteen then. I was thirty-five. He's twenty-eight now. Almost as old as I was that midnight, when we were wearily waiting for the plane to Phoenix. How long ago was that? Almost fifteen years.

"I'm sorry, son."

"What for?"

"That you've got such a long wait."

"You're comforting me, as though I was the one who'd had his heart stitched up!"

That *textile* image "stitched up" surprised me. As I thought about it, language became the only reality, I felt that every physical touch was freed of pain, and that was a nice illusion.

I'm really well, I feel cheerful and it's easy to forget I've had my heart "stitched up."

Other than a dull ache in the vein they opened in my groin, in that soft area between my genitals and my thigh . . .

When I was lying on the operating table, at a certain moment I had become aware of that, that they were shaving my groin; a cold and quite disagreeable touch. At the time I didn't know why they were doing it. If my problem is my heart, I thought, why are they shaving my private parts?

A cold razor blade scraping over my skin.

And the image of a man condemned to death, being prepared in the morning for the electric chair, came suddenly to my mind.

And then this: Today Sanja said that was it. No more cigarettes.

"If you want to go on living," she said, "you have to stop."

And it was high time.

"There's a Bosnian, a doctor in Kentucky. I heard this story today. He had a heart attack, just like you, and while he was still in the hospital, he asked his wife to park the car behind the hospital building. Then he'd go out, hide in the car, and smoke a cigarette. Imagine! A doctor. His unfortunate wife refused to bring cigarettes, and she told his doctor colleagues about it."

In America everything is geared to stopping you smoking. Of all the nations on the planet, they are the most resistant to the tobacco habit.

Nevertheless, one of the finest sentences about the cigarette and dependence on it was written by an American, Laird Hunt: "When you smoke, other people come up to you and ask for a light."

The next day.

I thought about how the news of her son's heart attack could upset my mother in Bosnia. To preempt any possible pain, I called her and explained that a rumor I had had a heart attack was likely to spread through the Bosnian part of the world. I was calling, I said, so that my voice and cheerfulness would reassure her that this was not the case.

She listened to me attentively, then there was a short pause before she asked: "So how are you, otherwise?"

I clearly recognized her anxiety in that *otherwise*.

"Of all possible diseases, they hit on a heart attack," she said. "The Mehmedinovićes don't have them. No one in the family either on your father's side or on mine has ever had a problem with their heart."

So, that meant I was the first. Genetic degeneration had to start with someone; or else I—like all my relations—had started out with the same inherited heart, only I had carelessly filled mine with stuff that exceeded its capacity.

And when the call was over, I remembered a line of verse I had last thought about perhaps in the late 1970s. It wasn't remotely worthy, metaphysical poetry, but a rudimentary line by the forgotten Bosnian poet Vladimir Nastić, that went: "I swooned, Mother, like you, giving birth to me."

Sanja came this morning before eight o'clock. On her way to my ward, she had bought me a decaf in the hospital canteen. The decaf was sweetened with artificial sweetener.

It wasn't coffee, it wasn't sugar, nor was I myself.

And she said: "You're looking well!"

I nodded affirmatively, clearly I looked well, tied to the bed with all these cables so that I couldn't move, sit up, or get out of bed and walk around the room. But that didn't bother me. And I drank the coffee with great pleasure, just as though it were real coffee, with natural white sugar.

And then my phone rang. I saw a familiar number, I picked it up, and from the other end I heard a strange sound like human breathing. I spoke, but the caller couldn't hear me. I listened for a while and finally recognized the sound of a man moving. The mobile's microphone was picking up the sound of rubbing against the material inside his pocket.

Sanja asked: "Who is it?"

"No one."

"So why are you listening?"

"I'm listening to the direct broadcast of human being walking."

This morning a new nurse came. She said it would be good for me to move, to walk around the room. I instantly dug myself out of bed, still plugged into hundreds of wires, and with needles in my veins.

In the bathroom, Sanja carefully washed my whole body with a wet cloth.

Then I walked around the room. It was good to be walking again. This was what the experience of one's first step was like. I was walking!

But afterward, I was sitting in my chair and suddenly straightened up, and at that moment I felt something burst in my right groin (where they had shaved my private parts the day before with a razor). At the same moment I saw a swelling appear in that place. I pressed the button on my bed to call the nurse, who came quickly and looked at the swelling with interest. She measured my penis, which was lying over the swelling, with the outside edge of her hand and looked. She was concerned, she measured the pulse in my feet and hurried out of the room to find the duty doctor.

Very soon, instead of her and the doctor, a young man

appeared, a technician with a strange plastic object. In the center of the square object was a half ball, which he pressed onto the swelling. The ends of the flat board into which the ball was incorporated had holes with a paper string drawn through them. He tied the string around my waist. But he moved slowly, all the time reading the instructions for installing this plastic object whose purpose was, presumably, to read impulses or messages sent by the swelling near my genitals.

And it wasn't working. He gave up. He laid the plastic object down on the bedside cabinet, and left.

Was I now supposed to act like someone ill?

I didn't want to.

No.

In Chekhov's diaries there is a short note, a sketch for a story, about a man who went to the doctor, who examined him and discovered a weakness in his heart.

After that the man changed the way he lived, took medicines, and talked obsessively about his weakness; the whole town knew about his heart, and all the town's doctors (whom he consulted regularly) talked about his illness. He didn't marry, he stopped drinking, he always walked slowly and breathed with difficulty.

Eleven years later, he traveled to Moscow and went to see a cardiologist. That was how it emerged that his heart was, in fact, in excellent shape. To begin with, he was overjoyed at his health. But it quickly turned out that he was unable to return to a normal way of life, as he was completely adapted to his rhythm of going to bed early, walking slowly, and breathing with difficulty.

What's more, the world became quite tedious for him, now that he could no longer talk about his illness.

A young African man had come to photograph my heart.

(On his index finger, rather than on his ring finger like most people, he had a silver ring with a square stone, that is, a combination of two stones: a large turquoise in the form of a tear was integrated into a square of black onyx; for the next half hour, as I watched him work, I looked at that ring.)

To photograph my heart, he used a handheld scanner and moved the cold, egg-shaped object, on the left side of my naked chest, over my breastbone. On the monitor in front of him, was he focusing on the image of my heart? Or some other visual content? I don't know, I couldn't see what he was seeing. I always felt a bit dizzy whenever I heard my own heart. For some reason, I don't like to hear that sound, which means that I don't like hearing the ticking of ancient clocks, either. My hand sometimes falls unconsciously onto my chest, on the left side, just as I am falling asleep, then I become aware of my heart, and that wakes me up. And now, as that young man was recording me, I was seething with discomfort. At one moment he pressed the round scanner hard down between my ribs. This was a moment of utter bodily discomfort.

"What are you doing?"

"I'm trying to make a bit of space between your ribs, so that I get a clearer image."

I can easily handle pain.

But this wasn't pain; this was separating the ribs right by the heart, this was far more than I was prepared to put up with. And that pressure between my ribs unleashed an uncontrollable fury in me. He had been scanning for half an hour already—had he taken any images? He said he had, but that it wasn't enough. And I told him that for me what he had already recorded was absolutely enough. I pulled my pajamas over my chest, and crossed my arms over it for good measure, to prevent any further approach to my ribs.

It was as the young man, confused by my reaction, was putting away the instrument and leaving the room that Sanja appeared with a decaf in a cardboard cup. She noticed my agitation and asked—what happened? I waved my hand, never mind, nothing, the examination took too long and that's why I was irritated. But then, I was put out by the expression on the young man's face. While he was packing up his apparatus, there was a smile of mild revolt on his face. Did he think I was a racist? That was it! I could see it in his expression. That's what he thought. He thought I reacted the way I did not because I didn't enjoy having him forcing my ribs apart, but because I had something against the color of his skin. I felt a need to talk to him, to set the record straight, but I knew that could only increase the misunderstanding.

So I didn't say anything.

Nor did he.

He left without a word.

Then Sanja told me my friends were calling and they wanted to visit me in the hospital.

No, no.

They wanted to assure themselves that the heart attack had happened to me, and not to them. That was human and normal, they wanted to confront the confirmation that the misfortune had passed them by.

No way.

I refused.

I didn't want anyone to visit me in the hospital.

The third day.

I was moved out of intensive care into an ordinary hospital ward, where I shared a room with this old man. He was a Slovak by origin.

Lukas Cierny.

That's what was written in blue felt-tip on a little board on the wall, to the right of his bed. Nice name. Lukas Cierny.

How old could he be? Eighty? Maybe more.

He had Alzheimer's disease, and some chest problems, and his breathing was very restricted.

In the middle of the night he got out of bed and set off somewhere, and they brought him back from the corridor.

"Where were you going?"

"I want to get dressed and go for a walk."

Old Cierny is much loved, there's a procession all day long of his children, grandchildren, and great-grandchildren. They fill our room with laughter while they fix their father's, grandfather's, or great-grandfather's pillows under his head; comb the sparse hairs on his skull; and do whatever they can to please him. It's clear from the old man's vacant gaze that he doesn't know who all these people are. They turn to me as well, kindly, as though we'd always known one another and were related. The mere fact that I came from a Slavic part of the world gave them the right to that familiarity. Even though their own Slavic origin was pretty foreign to them. His daughter, when she introduced herself to me, said of Lukas: "He's from Czechoslovakia." She was a pure-blooded American, from Pennsylvania.

He, who remembered nothing anymore, answered questions in English and then sometimes in Slovak. When he replied in Slovak, the people he was talking to didn't understand him. However, that didn't bother any of them, they weren't conversing with him to exchange information, but to simulate communication.

Someone had just come into the room and greeted Lukas with "How you doin'?"

To which he replied: "*Dobro.*"

It was a reflex response in Slovak, a language that at this time was evidently closer to him. The person to whom the old man directed his *dobro* didn't understand the word. The old man had been separated from his Slovak language for some seventy years. And now the word came out of him, as it were, unconsciously. But this linguistic muddle had an emotional effect on me. As though now, close to death, the old man was preparing to face death in *his own* language. When he pronounced his *dobro* it confirmed for me that I was in a foreign, distant land. That was a most unusual experience of language.

Sanja was sitting by my bed, and when she heard the old man say *dobro*, as though in our shared language, her eyes automatically filled with tears.

Lukas Cierny looked like the Bosnian poet Ilija Ladin.

It wasn't just a matter of physical similarity. Ladin, too, suffered from complete amnesia before his death.

But now, when I thought about him, the way he appeared in my memory, I became aware that Ladin had many faces.

I remembered: In a box of his photographs, there were lots taken in those express photo booths, which you rarely see nowadays, in the streets of towns all over the world. In a matter of seconds, the machine would make four shots, four portraits on a square of cheap photographic paper. Ilija went into those booths in Paris, Milan, Sarajevo, and other towns, and had his photograph taken as a souvenir. In the pictures, his portrait was repeated four times, but in each one his expression was different, and with each new expression, he was a different person.

Before his death, as I said, he suffered from complete amnesia. He was put into an old people's home. His friends brought him books he had written, which he looked at as though he'd never seen them before. He couldn't recognize himself in the photograph of the author printed on the cover.

In our room, now, Lukas Cierny was breathing with difficulty, as though having an asthma attack. That lasted for a while, and then he calmed down, and I no longer heard his breathing. And each time that happened, I thought he had died.

Not to remember, is that a punishment? Or a blessing?

In the course of the evening, the nurses who looked after the two of us changed.

That evening there was an African Muslim girl here, wearing a violet silk scarf, with full makeup, including bright red lipstick, as though she were going out for the evening, to a restaurant and not a hospital ward. She was quite cheerful and sweet, young. She may have been twenty, perhaps twenty-five, but she addressed me and the old man with whom I shared a room as though we were children.

"Where are you from?" I asked.

She laughed, and asked back: "Where do you think?"

"Ethiopia?"

"Close."

"Sudan."

"Close," she said, and waited for the guessing game to go on. But I didn't feel like going on guessing, so, disappointed at my faint-heartedness, she admitted: "Somalia."

She stood in front of the board—on which she was going to write her name and mine—and asked, with a felt-tip in her hand: "What's your name?"

After a brief hesitation, I replied: "Me'med."

From the perspective in which we found ourselves, the differences that are so fundamental to us became unimportant: whether she was from Sudan or Somalia. That mattered only to her, it left the entire continent where she now lived—indifferent. And the entire cosmos was indifferent to the differences in our identities. Seen from the perspective of death, it was a matter of total indifference which of the two of us was Slovak and which Bosnian, Lukas and Me'med, two patients stuck in the same room.

✦

Just before midnight (she had come into our room to take blood samples), the young Somali girl asked the old Slovak: "What's your name?"

He said nothing.

She asked: "And what year is this?"

And he said: "1939!"

That's what he said: 1939.

What did 1939 mean to him? He must have been ten, perhaps fifteen, then. That was the year before the big war. Maybe that was when he had to leave his home for good, and now, in his old age, it turned out that he had never left that year. Truly, what had happened to him in 1939? I would have liked to hear his story, but he was no longer in a state to tell it.

There's a year in my past I've never left as well.

1992.

Sometimes I'm woken by the clattering of Kalashnikovs over Sarajevo. I get up, make coffee, and stay awake till morning, through the window I look at the lights of Washington, or snow falling over the Pentagon.

During the night, Lukas Cierny got out of bed, and the young Somali put him back: "Where were you going?"

He replied: "To get dressed, I must go for a walk."

He didn't actually know he was in a hospital.

Then in the morning, when she was encouraging us to get out of bed, he refused, and she ordered him loudly: "Get up! Stand up!"

"No!" said the old man.

And then—over the old Slovak who was refusing to get out of bed—she began to sing: "Get up, stand up, stand up for your rights!" Youth is beautiful in its arrogance.

The young Somali girl, with her violet scarf, with her new makeup, gleamed in the morning light, bending over the Slovak at the end of his life. She was happy because she was at the end of her shift and singing.

I was waiting very impatiently to be let out of the hospital.

In fact, I was afraid this wouldn't happen today. It was Friday, and that would mean I'd have to stay here over the weekend.

But the doctor did appear, he asked me to walk down the corridors hooked up to all those sensors and sonars. I walked down the corridors, while the doctor followed the behavior of my heart on the monitor in front of him. I enjoyed that walk: in an hour I'd be outside, beyond the hospital walls.

When I came back into the room, the doctor checked the working of my heart once again, this time with a stethoscope, and as he didn't find any sinister sounds in my chest, in the end he gave me precise instructions on how to behave—when I got out of the hospital.

And then I could go home.

I looked at him. He was Indian, he was called Rayard.

And I thought: This man saved my life and we're parting like complete strangers.

I said: "You saved my life."

He said: "Yes."

And left.

After that, a smiling middle-aged man with a mauve bow tie ("I'm your limo driver") arrived and took me in a wheelchair through the corridors to the main entrance. This was a hospital ritual: regardless of the fact that I could walk, a man I had never seen before was pushing me in a wheelchair out of the hospital. There was something childish in that ritual move out of the world of the sick into the world of the healthy.

I parted from the stranger warmly, as though we had always known each other, and was left alone in front of the hospital. The fresh November air startled me. I was impatient to leave the hospital in which they had followed the behavior of my body for twenty-four hours on monitors and watched over my health. And, now that I was deprived of all that, on the street, waiting for my taxi, I felt a mild uncertainty, and fear.

Not every return home is the same.

When you come back from a journey, you find things just as you left them at the moment of departure. After all the days of being away, you are now back in your own room, perhaps there's an ashtray on the desk with a cigarette butt in it, perhaps a half-finished glass of wine, or a book you were reading on the day you left, open. Everything that retains a living trace of your presence in these objects becomes an image of the time that has passed and cannot ever be replaced.

I came back from the hospital and the first thing I saw from the doorway was the nice bedspread on the bed, the one with the floral design à la Paul Gauguin, which had come home before me. Washed, it lay over the bed, and it was unchanged, its textile essence was unchanged, there was no trace on it of the hospital, or of my illness.

Sanja had carefully removed from all the rooms most traces I had left of the rituals of my daily life, my previous life. She had taken particular care to eliminate the traces of those rituals that, according to the doctors' instructions, I ought to give up. There were no ashtrays, the smell of tobacco smoke had altogether vanished from the air.

I went into the sunroom, my covered balcony, my office.

I wasn't there either.

Erased from my rooms, now I could start over.

And then, reluctantly, I went into the bathroom, where it all began.

In our human habitations the bathroom is, apart from anything else, a place of fear, it is where we are naked and unprotected. That is why American films choose the bathroom as an emblematic theme of horror.

I undressed and stood in front of the mirror. I looked at the swelling on my right side, beside my genitals. It was no longer a swelling, but a bruise that was growing pale, with reddish edges, almost the color of rust.

I shaved.

Then I stepped cautiously into the shower, listening to the behavior of my body. The water was too hot. There was no pain in my neck, no pressure in my chest. Nothing hurt. The bathroom filled with warm steam. Water poured over me; was there anything simpler than this? A naked body with water pouring over it.

And I remembered a short film called *The Room*.

There was a long scene of bathing in it. A body with water pouring over it.

This is the story: A young man walks down the street as the light is fading, and through the open window of a room, above him, he hears the sound of a piano. And he stops. Then he sees the silhouette of the girl who was playing the piano. But the reason he stops is not *only* the music he heard or *only* the girl whose silhouette he saw. He doesn't know where the attraction comes from, he doesn't know the reason for his stopping, but he is aware of a strong magnetic pull from that room, sensed through the open window. And years pass. He leaves that town and lives all over the world, then as an old man he returns. He buys an apartment and lives out his last years in it. After bathing, he leaves his room and hears the siren of an ambulance stopping in front of his building. It is night. And then he becomes conscious of everything. The room where he now finds himself is the room he had once seen, as a young man, while the sound of a piano reached him through the open window. And why had he felt such a strong attraction? The young man could not have known what the old man knew now: what he had seen then was *his* room, the one in which, when the time came, he would die.

I came out of the shower; wrapped in a towel, I walked through the whole apartment. Now I'm looking out the window, and I say: "This is not *that* room."

Sanja hears me. She stands behind me, leaning her head against my wet back, and asks: "What did you say?"

RED BANDANA

Somewhere in Virginia, I lost my cap.

—JOHN CAGE

Dear Son,

Last Thursday I went for a routine six-month checkup at the doctor's. I would like to free myself from the medication I have been taking for nearly five years now, which makes me tired and slows me down. I want to speed up, to run, because I want to get back into my life. The doctor, a young Sikh with a pale mauve turban, said: "No, no. The medication is to prevent a heart attack." I know, I say, but I would like to free myself of its side effects, and I'll worry about a heart attack in a different way. He assures me that the side effects of this medication are innocuous in comparison to its positive effects on my organism. I ask: "And, in fact, what are its real side effects?" He says there are several, but none of them kill you. "For instance?" "Well, say, *memory loss*." "Does that mean I could forget everything?" "Yes, but forgetting doesn't kill you," says the cardiologist. I ask: "If I forget everything, my whole life, if I can't recognize my child's face, if I forget my own name, isn't that the same as dying?"

After the checkup, driving home, I thought: What if I've already begun to forget? I looked for signs of my forgetfulness. But—how extensive is my forgetting? That can't be measured. What's forgotten is now inaccessible because it's invisible, because it's in "the darkness of oblivion." Then I felt the need to be in the company of a person with whom I had shared a lot of time in the past, so as to compare our memories of the same events. I was looking for a way of returning to my past, and so, the same day, I bought a plane ticket to Arizona. And maybe the conversation with the doctor was just an excuse for something that I had been planning for years—going back to see our apartment in Phoenix again, our first American address.

And two days later, on 16 April 2015, I flew to the other side of the continent. Over the last week, during my journey, I wrote this diary, which is probably only of any importance to me. But it might be important to you, too, because it is written for just one reader, you. It was vital for me to hide a few sentences that I wanted to say to you, here, among a mass of others. And you will find them easily. If you don't find them, that will mean that you haven't read it. And that's always a possibility lying in store for every text: to remain unread. Books are lonelier than people.

I flew Delta. In March 1996, at the airport in New York, a woman told me: "Since the breakup of the Soviet Union, Delta airplanes serve to carry packets of banknotes to Russia and to bring gold back to the U.S." Over the last twenty years, whenever I flew with Delta I remembered that woman and the Russian gold. I looked around, there were still ashtrays on the back of the aircraft seats, admittedly screwed up so they couldn't be opened, smoking has been banned for a long time. Judging by the ashtrays, this plane had been flying in the early nineties, maybe even to Moscow.

But the flight from Washington to Phoenix lasted barely four hours. Allowing for the two-hour time difference, it turned out that I had flown west for a little more than an hour (the plane left at 6:00 and landed at 7:20 a.m.). I rarely travel north or south. The journey west can start at night, but for me for some unknown reason it's connected with the morning. Which means that I always feel that dawn has just broken when I fly toward the west. While moving east is always connected with weariness and I drift off to sleep in my seat in broad daylight, as though it were a night flight. That's how it is when I travel from the East to the West Coast of America; it's the same when I fly from America to Sarajevo and back.

♦

Phoenix airport. The first thing I saw when I came into the parking lot was the red bandana around your head.

For the next five days we were going to wander aimlessly along American roads. Wander aimlessly? That means feeling the real proximity of the world and being aware of oneself, of one's body in space. Back in the nineties, you remember, we drove without a map through the minor country roads of Virginia, with the idea of getting lost, and then searching for a road that would take us home. To wander means to confront a simple, healing truth: the world is bigger than I am! Aimlessness was the only purpose of our journeys, even though we moved farther from home with every second. Although that could be a definition of home, too: it's always wherever you're in the company of those closest to you.

A red bandana. My gran, your great-grandmother, used to wear a similar scarf on her head. Hers was white, but it seems to me that it had the same pattern on it as the bandana on my son's head.

The first time we landed at this airport, on 1 February 1996, our luggage didn't arrive with us. It got lost somewhere along the way. The airport official said it wasn't a problem and that, as soon as it arrived, they would forward our suitcase to our address. But at that point we didn't have an address. The luggage was lost, and that filled me with indescribable anxiety. Later it turned out that the contents of our suitcase were quite inconsequential: some winter clothes that we wouldn't need in the desert and books that, in all probability, we wouldn't read again. But because we were refugees from a war, that suitcase was our entire property, it was our all.

✦

Today, when we reached the door of our old apartment (the address at which twenty years before, our suitcase had arrived a week late), we were met by a young man, a caretaker or the director of the complex. He was agitated, possibly a bit afraid of our presence, he asked us not to hang around, and added: "Don't take any photographs!" Something had happened here. After I explained our reasons, pointing at the door of the apartment where we had lived twenty years earlier and after he was convinced that we had not come with any evil intentions, he said: "You can stay for five minutes, but you can't take any pictures."

There was a blue canvas chair by the door, quite faded by the sun, and an empty beer bottle . . . The place looked abandoned, I thought no one lived behind that door. But then a man appeared in the doorway. He startled me because his face looked somehow familiar. I explained at once that we used to live here. Clint, the man was called. He understood the sentimental reasons for our visit, but when I asked whether we could take a photograph of us all together, he drew his head into his shoulders, looking at us suspiciously. He let me take our photo on my cell phone, but later, when we were already in the parking lot, he did after all let himself be photographed with me, hidden behind sunglasses. Something terrible had happened here, but I didn't ask what, and in fact I wasn't interested. I had just needed one minute standing in the silence in front of our apartment door, as in front of a mirror.

When we were alone, Harun said: "Did you see? Clint looks like you, you could be twins."

Today Phoenix looks like a city from the future. Over the last twenty years, there has been new building all around, and meanwhile it's only our apartment block that has begun to collapse. But Harun doesn't see it like that. The complex has remained a genuine poor ghetto, he says, the difference is that we came here from a war, at that time this was a great luxury for us. In February 1996, there was an orange tree growing in the yard, and after the hunger, mud, and ice, that was a heavenly contrast: the aroma of orange blossom came in through our window at night. He's right. My nostalgia (nostalgia?) had grown on an idealized and inaccurate image. Most of the people in the block at that time were Bosnians. The traces of war were still fresh: one young man in a camouflage uniform had a drum set with a lot of cymbals in his apartment and the noise of it was the soundtrack of our American exile; above us lived an old man who used to hold to his ear a plastic transistor radio with a bunch of batteries stuck to it with Scotch tape and at night he would climb onto the roof of our building to catch long-wave Radio Bosnia and Herzegovina; in the apartment opposite ours, while the children were eating watermelon in one room, their father hanged himself in another . . . I could go from door to door like this. Instead of Bosnians, other dead souls now live here.

And it all happened too fast: twenty years later, we entered the atrium of the building where we once lived, spent just a few minutes outside the door of our former apartment, because our arrival had disturbed the inhabitants and managers of the complex, so we left quickly. I don't know what else to say. And I don't feel good, it's as though I've been driven out of my own past.

There isn't an orange tree by the entrance anymore, they've planted palms instead.

✦

Our "return home" was supposed to be an important encounter with my own past, but in fact nothing occurred, apart from the coincidental oddity that our old apartment was now occupied by my "double." And I don't know how alike Clint and I really are, but I would like to believe in Harun's explanation, although he probably exaggerated that similarity to give our visit a particular symbolic meaning. But isn't that quite something in itself? Didn't I come here to confront myself, convinced that we don't in fact ever entirely leave the places where we've lived, some trace of us remains, our enduring presence, the way hotel mirrors retain the faces of all the people who have passed through the room? But it's never like that. We remember the place where we once lived, but it doesn't remember us.

And for a moment I believed again that it was nostalgia that had brought me here. But no. It was mere curiosity. While nostalgia is an emotion I connect with a concrete time: my late childhood, that sensitive adolescent phase when we have an infinite number of paths before us, but a few years later, when we reduce our choices to one, we feel a yearning for the time in which we could have chosen from among many different possibilities. That's nostalgia for me.

✦

Twenty years ago, as I drove to work in the morning, I would always glance to the left at the large brick-colored hill (Camelback Mountain) that reminds one of a camel's hump and gives its name to the street where we then lived, just to be sure that the castle was still there. Someone had built a real medieval fortress that looked unnatural in this desert landscape, like a geographical misunderstanding, like an optical illusion . . .

Today, twenty years later, we were driving uphill, toward the castle, along narrow serpentines between villas, and then—in front of one of the gates, we caught sight of a stone sculpture of the Buddha adorned with gold chains. It had probably been dressed like this by children playing. The sculpture of a smiling (hip-hop) Buddha going to fetch water. A thirsty Buddha. I left him my bottle of tonic water and we went on our way. Buddha, admittedly, is not God, but that is just how God should behave. And as we drove toward the top of the mountain, I thought about the fact that God's, Jehovah's, and particularly Allah's greatest shortcoming was that they were not prepared to let children decorate them or play with them in other ways.

The castle is being renovated. We saw its gate and walls from close up. But, sitting on its outer wall beside the steep road, I was able calmly to view the panorama of the city. Seen from above, the city itself seemed to me hidden: low buildings, stunted palms in a valley. Had it not been for a few skyscrapers in the center, I would have thought this wasn't a city. It's only at night, when the lights come on and stifle the stars in the sky, or become reflections of them, that the city reveals itself.

I was sitting on the low stone wall and looking from a height down onto a landscape in the valley that ought to have been familiar to me, but in fact it was quite alien. Why was I expecting to see a familiar scene from this height?

We hadn't been here long enough to have integrated into the space, so that this landscape would remember us. We lived here for not quite five months, it's our distant past now, and my most intense impression is connected with the heat of the desert. It's an artificial city, it couldn't survive without the water that is constantly poured over it, sprinklers poke up everywhere in grassy areas, activated from time to time so as to spray the surrounding earth. But nevertheless, the grass is always scorched. Phoenix is perpetually thirsty. In my memory the city is connected with Dalí, with that surrealist painting of his with the melting watches. Here, in the searing summer months, all the plastic parts of the cars melt. And all the vehicles look like that, as though the plastic parts had been patiently melted, forcibly, with cigarette lighters; the plastic slides downward, over the control panel behind the steering wheel. I remember warnings printed on VHS tapes from the video store, that they should not be accidentally left in the car, because the cassette would melt in the heat and then no longer serve its purpose. Dalí's watches, yes. It is said that time flows. In other cities time flows, but only in Phoenix does time melt.

In the 1990s there were no houses here, only a network of freshly asphalted roads. Between the roads, low desert plants and cactus grew. It's interesting, in recent years I have often dreamed about this terrain, although I don't understand why such a desolate landscape as Camelback Mountain should have left such a deep impression on my subconscious.

In one dream the Slovene poet Tomaž Šalamun is a real estate agent in a panama hat and gray linen suit, very crumpled where the soft material easily creases, at the knees and elbows. He's showing me the reddish earth and cactuses beside the road and trying to persuade me to buy a house. I say: "But, Tomaž, there's no house here!" And he, as though expecting that reaction of mine, has his answer ready and says: "Plant tobacco! Plant tobacco!"

Where the Safari Hotel I worked in from February to June 1996 used to be, there is now a broad avenue of restaurants and shops, and on its sidewalk a man in a Hawaiian shirt is playing a trumpet loudly and atonally, so that passersby give him a wide berth . . .

"Oh, it's you, angry bird!"

So, in other words, something has survived of "my" hotel!

In the hall there had been a large cage, with a parrot in it, and it was forbidden to touch the bars because of the bird's dangerous beak, and whenever it shrieked in a voice that ricocheted off the marble walls, the horrified guests would hurry to take refuge in their rooms.

✦

We're driving north. Harun is talking about a local film fes-
tival that has just closed, still affected by something that had
happened there. The projection of a film by an acquaintance
of his was supposed to have taken place the previous evening, but there was something wrong with the video and the
image refused to be projected onto the screen. The organiz-
ers had tried to "open" the video in a different format, but
it didn't work. The images refused to start moving and no

one knew why. For the rest of the evening other films were shown without a hitch. And this morning, that acquaintance of his, the unfortunate film producer, went out for his usual morning exercise and died. He was on his bicycle when death came.

We're on Route 17, rare drops of rain have started falling, and I want a strong black coffee.

Father and son. When I'm stuck for words in an argument with you, I say: "I know what the world looked like before you were born."

You can't remember this. In the hospital, I'm looking at you through a glass wall: you were born the night before and the nurse is changing your diaper. First I see your naked, vulnerable little body, and then I recognize my crooked nose on your face. That nose. My nose. Duplication. My solitude has just been dizzyingly diminished.

At night, when you're driving and need someone to talk to, you call me. And then we talk. We live in different time zones, there's three hours' difference between us, it's midnight, or past midnight where I am, but you know that I'm awake and working, reading or writing. Whenever this happens, when you call, I become aware of my solitude. And of your solitude. We talk, we encourage each other, we breathe into our telephone receivers, alone in the void of the cosmos.

When we reached Arcosanti, the evening light was breaking on the tips of the larches and cupolas of the experimental town. In the parking lot in front of us, a small girl on a bicycle was riding in a circle, completely immersed in her game. In a little blue dress, she was spinning around, until her father appeared and put an end to the bicycle pirouette by picking the child up with her small means of transport and hugging them to him, then they disappeared from our sight.

After we moved to Arizona in 1996, we visited this place, the primary concept of which was the connection between architecture and ecology (*arcology*). And now, twenty years later, I had to talk Harun into turning off the main road to come here to see how the settlement had changed in the meantime. The architect, Paolo Soleri, had died two years earlier. Half a century since the building began, the town is still not finished. We spent too little time there, because Harun was in a hurry, but I was nevertheless left with the impression of that *incompleteness*. This is how everything ought to be built, so that the process lasts indefinitely. That's how a book should be written, over a whole lifetime, and still unfinished. I would

like it if everything of mine was like this town, in a state
of constant youth.

✦

When we came out onto Route 40, Harun drove west for a
time and then stopped at the side of the road, turned off the
engine, and said: "Do you remember this place?"

Did I remember the 4 January 2005? We were traveling
from the East to the West Coast. When we reached Arizona,
the rain turned suddenly into a snowstorm. As soon as we saw
the exit for Flagstaff, we turned off the road and took a room
in the first motel we came to, with a window from which I
could watch the snow enveloping our car in the parking lot.

I managed to fall asleep, but sometime after midnight, you woke me and said: "Let's go, the Weather Channel says this is an unprecedented storm and the snow is going to completely cut the town off, but I have to be in Los Angeles tomorrow." Naturally I objected, but at that moment the power went off and you said: "You see?" We packed quickly, the elevator wasn't working, so we made our way down the stairs in the dark to the ground floor, woke up the receptionist, and signed out. The snow was dry, we raked it off the car roof with our hands. When we got out onto the road, you turned on your camera and photographed the roadway in front of us. Snowplows had cleared the city roads, but when we reached Route 40, all we had in front of us was a white expanse, with pine forests to the left and right of us. The snow was swirling, making miniature white tornadoes along the way. I drove slowly, I had the impression that we were no longer on the road but wandering over snowy meadows. But then a heavy truck appeared behind us and I slowed down to let it pass. After it overtook me, I followed its red brake lights, they were our compass in the snowstorm. And as long as we were driving uphill, everything was all right, the problems began when we started to go down, because the truck sped up. We sped up as well. Then I lost control of the steering wheel, the car began to turn vertiginously and gather speed, and I don't know how long it all lasted before we plowed backward into the snow on the right-hand side of the road. The engine died.

I remember my indescribable fear that we would be forever stuck in the snow, in the middle of the mountains. I turned the key, the lights went on in the car, and at that moment it was as though colors had returned to our world!

Ten years had passed; you stopped the car, we got out and crossed the road, and only then did I see that at its edge was a sheer drop. "We got off easy!" We looked into the abyss, and from under my shoes pebbles started rolling downhill.

But do you remember the snow in Sarajevo? In the winter of 1988, we took the cable car up Trebević Mountain. The road from the overlook was icy, but some rare cars passed us nevertheless. The snow was deep, we had brought a sled. The photograph taken at that time by the photographer from *Our Days* magazine is a reminder of the month in which I let my beard grow, for the first and only time in my life. We had met him on the way, before the path began to go downhill toward that mountain hut, whose name I've forgotten. Walking down the icy slope was more effort than sitting on the sled and letting it take us where we were headed. However, the road here runs along dangerous edges above steep drops, which I hadn't taken into account. The sled sped up dizzyingly, and I remember my inexpressible fear that a late vehicle could appear from the opposite direction. Sanja went silent, you covered your eyes with your little hands, while I had no choice, I hugged you to me and threw myself, together with the sled under me, to the right. I tore my jeans, Sanja injured her knee, and I think she hasn't forgiven me to this day. But had the sled taken us to the left, into the abyss, that photo of the little family in the snow would have been our last photo. And, I remember, that same evening, when we got home, I shaved off my beard.

We drive through Flagstaff. This is the town where Harun lives now. I want to stop, to see his apartment, to look around the district where he lives. Simple curiosity. But he refuses. "It's not important," he says. It's more important that we should reach the desert as soon as possible in order for him to photograph the night sky in time, because the map of clouds on his mobile forecasts rain before midnight. He's a photographer. And I like his pictures. But there's something natural in my wish to get to know the area where he lives. If he had come to my new address, I would have been glad to show him the place, because I think that the space where we live redefines us, shows us changed, the way we are now. That's why I want to see what he is like *now*. "I want to see the view from your window," I say. And he raises his arm irritably from the steering wheel, points at the glass pane in front of us, and says: "That's my window!"

We drive through Flagstaff. For some reason, all the events connected with this town have the flavor of a dream. This occurred in the winter of 2008, I was working for Reuters at the time. I came to work, put my knapsack down on my desk, and then from the studio I heard alarmed fragments of a report about an atomic attack. Soon afterward I learned that terrorists had dropped a nuclear bomb on Flagstaff, Arizona. My first thought was: Why Flagstaff? And then, interested in the news, I got up and went into the studio as though hypnotized. And there on the monitors the program was live, a reporter in Arizona was describing the consequences of the attack. Experts on terrorism were sitting in the studio, and all those faces were familiar to me from the broadcasts of the big television channels. And then I realized: this was all set up, it was an exercise run by a team from the Ministry of Homeland Security, which rented our studio from time to time to record their programs.

At one moment, one of the producers noticed the appearance of a foreigner (me), came up to me, and said: "Who are you? What are you doing here?"

"I'm from here," I said, pointing to the archive, my windowless room. "I'm interested in the news from Arizona," I said.

He asked me politely to leave and then closed the door, and I believe that he locked it. I was quite unnerved: the reporter's dramatic voice, the aggressive graphics accompanying the living images, the names under the people speaking, and so on, that was all real television, I thought. The recorded program about this "nuclear attack" could one day be shown as a real event, live, in some future now. And that was a fairly troubling thought.

In the passenger seat, I endeavored to fall asleep. It was not yet midnight. The phone rang. Aleš from Ljubljana. I said I was traveling. I explained the reasons for our journey. I said that we were parked in the dark somewhere on the border between Arizona and Utah and that I felt as though I had gotten lost on my way home. I didn't know where I was.

He laughed, and then explained: "In English they say 'home, sweet home,' while we say 'Love home, wherever it is.' In principle, no one can call an American's home into question, so he can simply state that 'home is sweet,' while it's different for us, for us the existence of a home is always questionable: you can love your home only if you have one."

Clever Aleš. At the end of 1996, he was our first acquaintance from Europe to visit us in America. We were already in Washington then, still young thirty-five-year-olds. He arrived with a virus, stayed a few days, largely treating himself by putting drops of propolis on lumps of sugar. Do you remember propolis drops? A winter medicine from bees at the time of Yugoslavia. The last time I saw a little bottle of propolis was that week when Aleš Debeljak stayed with us.

And suddenly the car filled with the scent of an Alpine plant!

Aleš. We talked for a few more minutes. Outside the temperature dropped below zero. But stars could be seen behind the clouds.

✦

Monument Valley. Harun arranged his cameras in the dark and came back to the car. We sat in the van for hours gazing into the darkness. It had grown quite cold outside, late snow must have fallen somewhere nearby. I don't know what Harun was taking photographs of in the pitch dark. The camera lens sees more than the human eye. Sitting calmly in the driver's seat, he fell asleep for a few hours before dawn while I stayed awake till morning. It was only after daybreak that I caught sight of the amazing stone forms in the valley in front of us. So that's what our cameras were photographing all night? Those stone forms had been shaped by the wind. I got out of the car.

I sat down on a stone and looked at the sculptures that I had until then believed existed only as "matte paintings" in Ford's films, just a drawing in Italian cartoons, published in my childhood, and later in Harun's by Sergio Bonelli . . . A wind had gotten up from the north. I sat on the stone, watching. After all, the wind was a greater sculptor than Ivan Meštrović.

Well done, wind!

On the plateau from which we had been photographing the sky all night, just before morning a young Asian man, a photographer, appeared. I watched him putting the lenses on his camera in his white Toyota. Then he tied a flashlight around his head. It was not yet daybreak. He got out of his car into the darkness and, with a beam of red light from his forehead, set out into the desert. A unicorn. He had not been there at dawn. As far as the eye could see: desert, and not a single human shadow.

So, it was only after dawn that I became aware of the place where we found ourselves. I had not known that the desert was so beautiful. We like to ask ourselves metaphysical questions about the world, life, and man. But we ought to ask ourselves again and constantly: Why fill our lives with such effort and torment, when we know that we will be here only once and when we have such a brief and unrepeatable time in this indescribably beautiful world?

✦

The parking lot in front of the hotel is empty, but at reception a young Navajo claims that all the rooms are taken, apart from one special one that costs $380 a night. Impossible! That's outrageously expensive, I say. The parking lot is empty, but he insists that this is the only room. It can't be that this boy is punishing me because in his eyes I'm a white male, a tourist in his country. "Young man, I haven't slept for two nights, the hotel is empty, and I just want a bed where I can close my eyes!" He shakes his head, there aren't any empty beds. It's impossible that he sees me that way and is punishing me accordingly. And then I say: "Look at me, young man! I'm not white!" Drawn by our conversation, hotel workers begin to gather behind him, smiling awkwardly. I go outside. But how else can I say it? I'm not a white man! Always, on every continent, I'm an endangered minority. For Europeans, I'm Muslim. For Asians, I'm European. For Americans . . . I've been told several times here "Go back to Russia!" and that's the mildest form of identity rebuke. Why am I forever being punished for other people's sins? Always out in the open, with no shelter, prepared in advance for blows. And I carry with me the remnants of all the shells that have fallen on the houses where I have lived, like a confirmation of survival, and as a warning. That was a sudden, brief attack of self-pity. And do I have the right to self-pity, *in this place?*

I haven't slept for two nights, it's drizzling, I'm sadder than I'm prepared to admit. We're in a desert, the so-called high desert, and it's cold.

✦

I want to fall asleep in the comfort of a motel bed, but my son is against that, asking: What greater comfort is there than sleep under the open sky, under the stars? Not that long ago, on a journey like this one, a few hours before dawn, we fell asleep in this car in a parking lot somewhere in West Virginia. In the morning my neck was completely stiff. It's good that I quickly forget pain. I remember that I was in pain that morning. And I remember watching, barely awake, as a young man at dawn changed the text on the advertising board of the restaurant across the road. It was a large board on a high post, and he was skillfully using a long pole made for the purpose to place magnetic letters and arrange them into a short text, giving the price and menu for breakfast that day. It was a dreary day, and he was lifting up the letters, constantly gazing high up at the board, whose top touched a cloud. Watching him made me tired. And I thought: If I had to do his job, with the pain I was currently feeling, I would not have the strength to look up at the sky and place letters above my head. Letters had never seemed so heavy to me as then, that morning in a little town called Fayetteville.

At the entrance to the Monument Valley Navajo Tribal Park a car had just drawn up. An Indian man, with long hair tied in a ponytail, peered out of the little hut beside the entrance and tried to explain to the couple of gray-haired Americans in the expensive convertible with its roof down—unsuccessfully (because they kept insisting on additional clarification)—why the park was closed, and asked them to turn around and go back the way they'd come. He was getting tired of explaining and suddenly, in midsentence, he switched from English to his own native tongue . . . He talked, they listened although they didn't understand a single word. In fact, it was only now when they couldn't understand that they listened. And after that, mutual comprehension was established.

Today we drove through northern Arizona, westward, and I was tired so fell asleep in my seat. I hadn't slept for more than an hour, but, evidently under the influence of the previous night's conversation, I had a strange dream. In my dream, Aleš was driving me to the airport. "Your Ljubljana's lovely," I say. He smiles with pleasure. It's a sunny day. We stop at a car park outside a family home; on the left is an unusual tree, and a strange flower is growing from the middle of the trunk, with thick green resin running out of it. I watch Aleš using scissors to carefully cut the long stem of the red flower, which looks like a poppy. It's important that the resin doesn't touch the skin because it's poisonous. The flower is rare—he explains to me in the dream—and blooms only once in a hundred years. I ask what the tree is called. And he says: "Maple." And, as though justifying himself, he explains: "I need this flower for a new poem."

When I first wake, I have two mental windows through which I can look. One faces into reality, the other, backward, into the dream from which I have just woken. If the image from the dream is intense, that's the first thing I think of when I wake up, and that's why I remember the dream.

As he drives, when Harun lifts his left hand to the steering wheel, the little finger is separate from the rest of his hand, and the top is crooked. He had crushed that finger badly with the iron top of the water manhole in the courtyard. That had happened more than twenty years earlier. Do you remember that pain now? It was wartime, the hospitals were crammed with the wounded. We saved his finger with a mixture of herbs, a balm that had made a man by the name of Handžić famous. This balm had, allegedly, treated wounds throughout the long history of Bosnian wars, as far back as anyone could remember. I wrapped gauze around the "little warrior's" wound, and in the end it all turned out fine, apart from the fact that the finger had remained a little bent at the base of the nail.

You were always afraid of doctors. You were three, a rose thorn was stuck in the palm of your hand, I took you to a

clinic, where nuns happened to be working that day. You refused to go into the clinic, while they encouraged and cajoled
you. You resisted, screaming and arguing: "No, no!" Want-
ing to insult them, you shouted: "Penguins! Penguins!" And
the nuns laughed.

The scent of a three-year-old boy's hair has stayed in my
memory.

Page, Arizona. After two sleepless nights, here we are in a
hotel. I take a shower. I wait for the trickle of water to shift a
blue thread from my shirt that had settled in my navel.

Stretched out on the hotel bed, Harun is absorbed in the
photographs he has taken today, so that his laptop is constantly in danger of falling off the edge of the bed onto the
floor. That's how it always is with him, something is always
threatening to nose-dive off the edge of something . . .

I remember, he could have been three or four, I am holding him in my arms, but he's restless, he struggles in my embrace, and then succeeds in getting away and falls so that he
cuts his tender child's chin on the edge of the chair. As he
grew, the scar got bigger. He never reproached me for it,
maybe because men like their scars. But his mother, whenever she felt a need to put things straight, would scold me as
a joke: "Come on, don't flatter yourself, you weren't capable of
holding him even when he was a baby!"

✦

I was woken by the sound of the door opening. I sat up in bed and looked out the window at the mauve neon sign on the roof of the motel opposite us. For a moment I regretted being jolted out of my comfortable sleep. And I tried in vain to remember what I'd been dreaming about. I was woken by the sound of a door opening, and after I became aware of that sound, I looked automatically out the window, listening to all the sounds from outside. And so my dream vanished. If everyday reality is intensive, and if I think of it the moment I wake, I forget my dream. I was woken by the sound of a door opening. Awake, I looked out the window. I dragged myself out of bed and discovered that the door of our room was unlocked. I went out and surveyed the parking lot from the motel veranda. In the middle of the parking lot was a swimming pool surrounded by a high wall. The swimming season had not begun, there was no water in the pool, but around the empty egg-shaped hollow, there were several sun loungers. On one, a woman wrapped in a gray coat was sitting, rocking from left to right, as though soothing an inner pain. I watched the glow of her cigarette. A black jeep had just come into the parking lot, a man got out, set off toward the motel reception, but then stopped, changed direction, and went up to the pool wall. He stood right beside it, listening. He couldn't see the woman, and she couldn't see him. Only the wall separated them. In all probability, she was not aware of his presence. In the silence, the man laid his hand on the wall. Delicately, the way one lays one's hand on the belly of a pregnant woman, and as though attempting to discover through his open palm what was not accessible to his eyes. And that was all. Nothing else occurred. Exhausted from our journey, we had fallen asleep in a motel room with an unlocked door.

Lake Powell. While we were looking at the water from the shore, I took a photo of him with my cell phone. He's wearing my T-shirt. It used to please my father, too, when he saw me wearing a sweater of his ... My son's wearing my T-shirt and

I'm pleased with my photograph. I once asked Harun to take a photo of me, but so that the photograph made me look like a miner (as my father had been in reality). And he took photographs in which my face is the color of lead, and the pores on my face full of coal dust. I never asked him how he did it. But actually I don't want to know, because if he revealed his method to me, I might think that I didn't look authentic in those photos.

I like it here. Along the shore in front of us a girl walked by carrying an upside-down kayak over her, like an enormous yellow hat, which prevented us from seeing her head. In the distance is a thermoelectric wheel, with three stable semicircles like scoops of ice cream growing over it. This is an artificial lake. I know something about this. I grew up beside an artificial lake. Modrac. Tall dry grass along the shore rustled in the wind, and out of it disturbed pheasants flew in front of us. It was the artificiality of that lake that formed my melancholy. The water had filled up a valley, there were waves over the trees and the roofs of houses. And I remember the tips of poplars poking out of the water; we used to tie our rowing boats to their branches. My father would dive out of the boat and swim down, he wanted to see the foundations of his school under the water. That was where he had learned his first letters.

Modrac. I have a deep connection with my childhood, which was, put simply, happy, but I've very rarely written about it, because I've never mastered the skill of motivating myself to write about days filled with happiness. It's far easier to write about problematic events, about tragic and desolate days. When we arrived here, we had one email address, our whole three-member family: *Modrac@aol.com*. The word *modrac* was unknown to my new, and many of my old, friends, or they thought it just had some vague meaning connected with the color blue (*modro*). Few knew that it was the name of a lake, albeit an artificial one. I remember a misunderstanding from that time as well. A European acquaintance, a poet, on several occasions in his journalistic essays and articles, whenever he used my name, would also call me *mudrac* (wise man). At first I didn't know why, and then it dawned on me. "*Mudrac!*" He must have thought that's what *modrac* meant. He thought that I was calling myself a wise man by integrating that word into my email address. Horrendous! Others on the whole see us as we would not like them to see us. And the way others see us is the root of our shame.

The best photographs are always the ones we don't take. That's all right. Not everything has to end up as a photograph. What's most important needs to stay in the memory.

It was a sunny day, the road wound through a valley. The white line at the edge of the asphalt disappeared in the distance. We got out of the car to stretch our legs and to let Harun take some shots of the road. A fine uninhabited desert all around us. A slightly bitter aroma of plants. It was spring and the sky's gravity drew flowers and grasses up out of the earth. It was windy. Not a strong wind. A breeze. And then in front of us, down the slope of the road rolled a Ping-Pong ball. Where had it come from? Surely a puff of air could not have dislodged it from the stones by the roadway? It rolled briefly and came to rest in the low grass on the other side of the road. As though it had sensed an invisible human presence and for a moment there was terror in its movement. And I said: I know where this ball has come from! It's come here from May 1980. In the Botanical Garden at the Sarajevo National Museum, young employees were playing table tennis. I was woken that morning by the monotonous sound of their game. But then the ball got lost in the undergrowth by the fence, and after that, to my relief, silence fell again. The museum staff looked for it in vain. Among the local scrub, there is also endemic undergrowth from some other continent transplanted to the Botanical Garden at the Sarajevo National Museum, under the window of my student room at number 2 Franje Račkog.

We're driving. A car is an instrument of time. An aircraft can't be that. In a car, on the road, you're reduced to bare existence and the body is focused on real time. A plane is something else, a flight from one place to another is a violent contraction of time that completely interrupts your real experience of space. The two of us have often driven together from one coast of America to the other. I'm always bad-tempered be-fore a journey, but once I'm on the road, I relax and enjoy this constant succession of vistas. When I'm on the road I forget myself and become aware of the outside world . . . We're driving. No one is coming to meet us, just occasionally, across the road in front of us, the shadow of a bird passes.

There's a truck in front of us, pulling a horse trailer. It's dawn already. I watch dents being noisily thrust into the metal back of the trailer, the marks of the hooves of an agitated (or frightened) animal.

And to our right: Some soldiers, men and women, in green and brown camouflage uniforms, are slowly moving in all directions, all with their heads bowed, as though they are looking for a lost earring in the desert.

Harun has devised the plan of our journey, and he doesn't deviate from it. While we're on the road, there's not much we agree about, one of us is always on the verge of erupting. I ask him: "Must you have your way in everything?" I remember, some time before the war, the Sarajevo Youth Theater put on a performance of *Hamlet*, but the actors were children. My friend Kaća Čelan, who was directing the play, asked me whether Harun could act the young Hamlet (he must have been six or seven then). And when I later put her question to him, he replied: "No . . ." But then he changed his mind—he would, he would act, but only on the condition that he also directed the play! On our journey, everything had to be done his way. It was only when he brought me into the desert (Death Valley) that something in me calmed down, I stopped objecting, I began to enjoy the air, the food, everything . . .

An abandoned gas pump. There's nothing for miles all around, desert scrub and a cloudless sky. On the overgrown parking lot is a new red Ferrari with its roof down; the engine is off, but the key is there, and shoes are on the floor under the driver's seat. The building beside the pump is a ruin with no door, there's no one inside. There's desert all around and we wonder where the driver is. On the passenger seat is the March edition of *The New Yorker*. We both had the impression that someone was watching us. Something wasn't right. We got back into our car and drove on in silence for about half an hour, as though we were fleeing from the plot of a well-known American film, the name of which we couldn't remember. The previous week, in Arlington, while I was waiting for my appointment with the cardiologist, that same edition of *The New Yorker* was on the table, and I had read half the articles by the time it was my turn.

A campsite for caravans, arranged in a circle so as to form a small square in the center. A sandy square. It was already completely dark. On the square there was a thick beam of light, and a film projector was moving living images. A desert cinema for campers. We couldn't see what film was being shown, but we could hear its muffled sound: music and incomprehensible dialogue. The sound of the film merged with the voices of the audience.

The name of this place is the title of a film by Michelangelo Antonioni, *Zabriskie Point*. It's probably because Antonioni—or Sam Shepard, who wrote the screenplay for the film—was fascinated by the color of the terrain. Those pastel shades, hills that seemed to have been shaped by an ice-cream scoop, in various colors, strawberry and mint, banana and caramel . . . As I look at the hills, I feel the taste of cloud on my tongue. Zabriskie Point. The 1960s were the age of communes, dissatisfaction with the existing structures of society. The idea of escaping to the desert was appealing. To go where there was no one or where no one wished to go. But this is where Charles Manson escaped to as well, we saw the abandoned log cabin where he had lived, overgrown with dry desert grasses, his truck rusting in front. Escape is possible only as an individual act. Only an individual can escape. To escape as a group, even if into a desert, ends with one form or other of the problematic structuring of life in a human community. Manson himself asserted that even the smallest community tends toward a totalitarian structure and eventually ends in massacre. *Zabriskie Point* shows that escape is impossible, or that you can escape only alone, and only on the condition that you are not attached to other people, or possessions. And you know that. But what are you escaping from, my son?

At the gas station—Harun emptied a bag of ice into our blue plastic box in which we kept bottles of water and fruit juice. A pair of twins followed his every movement with great interest. They could have been three or four years old, the boy's hair was cut short, the girl had long hair the color of wheat (this is common in little girls from Nebraska or Iowa). But regardless of the obvious difference of their hairstyles, it was very easy to see their similarity. Twins. Harun cut the transparent bag with a knife, held it over the blue plastic box in which he had already placed several bottles of water, and scattered some of the bag's frozen contents over them. Then he put the bag down so that he could add more bottles to the box. After that he went back to the bag of ice. He carried out all these actions slowly and methodically, with great attention, taking care that not a single ice cube fell over the edge of the box onto the asphalt. The twins watched in wonder. And then, for some reason known only to a child's consciousness, they both simultaneously burst into tears. Their mother appeared from behind a large jeep and patiently, hugging them, took them one after the other back to their vehicle. She waved in our direction, as though apologizing for the children's crying, and then got into the vehicle herself. An attractive young mother, she had a yellow bandana tied around her neck.

It's exactly midnight! We are moving from 18 into 19 April. We got out of the car into the pitch darkness for you to show me the sky. And, truly, I had never seen so many stars above me. The night sky, provisionally speaking, is the only reliable scene to open to our eyes for thousands of years already. As I look at the stars, I become my own nameless forebear from the most remote past, who raised his head and saw, more or less, what I am myself seeing now from the darkness, in a place called Badwater Basin, 282 feet below sea level.

✦

Only once have I seen more stars in the sky. It was a winter night, January 1993, at midnight we left our apartment in the very center of Sarajevo, the city was in darkness, the icy cold froze the heart, but the sky was clear, studded with frozen stars. The sky above the Sarajevo valley had never been so open and bare as on that winter night, in a city without electricity. We stood and stared upward in astonishment, and my friend Ivan said, in his long, drawn-out Belgrade accent: "The staaarry sky above us, and moraaal laaaw within us!"

We've turned off the main road and now we're zigzagging along the tarmac. Harun is looking for a rise from which he can photograph the half-light in the desert basin and the sky above it. He is taking a time-lapse. We don't have an adequate expression for this in our language. I think that in our language, too, this method of taking and connecting photographs in a video would also be called time-lapse. Like the way in our language we use the word *makadam*. The word comes from McAdam, the name of the man who invented this kind of crushed stone for the stable body of a roadway. John Loudon McAdam. I remember that, in my childhood, our roads were spread with macadam. And I remember fear, because careless drivers would go too fast and scatter the little stones under their tires and hurt the children beside the road. This may have been true, but perhaps our mothers used that fear to keep us away from the roads. Lucia Berlin wrote a very short story called "Macadam." She writes about the joy of macadam that covered the red dust of the road out of her childhood in Texas. And at the end she says that she used to repeat *macadam* out loud, to herself, because the word "sounded like the name for a friend." And this is one of my deepest impressions from my early childhood, one of my earliest memories: I'm sitting on the wooden veranda of a house watching the road in front of it being spread with macadam. Then, as a cart pulled by a horse passed the digger with its sharp-edged metal shovel, there was a collision: the sharp metal tore the horse's leg, I saw its white bone, there was not much blood, the horse was shaking with shock and couldn't be calmed. And I feel the same sorrow half a century later, remembering it now.

The front bumper of Harun's pickup truck is broken, which makes it look mistreated and vengeful. Conscious of its threatening appearance, he abused it today on Artists Drive, a narrow one-way road that winds through the hills in the heart of Death Valley; he drove close behind a white Toyota Prius, which evidently alarmed its driver, who stopped to let us pass. In this country people are wary of trucks. The prejudice is that they are driven by white men from the interior, with a Confederate flag fluttering over their dusty vehicle. It's true that along our way we had seen many of those trucks with racist, usually anti-Obama stickers in their back windows. And we had seen one two days earlier from close up, on a blue Ford pickup parked beside Lake Powell: MUSLIMS GO HOME AND TAKE OBAMA WITH YOU!

In the desert, our right-hand front tire burst. Harun is changing the wheel. My camera is swaying on my chest, and from time to time I point it at him. He is evidently irritated by my taking photos of him working. "Last week," I say, "I was driving to my medical checkup, they were laying new asphalt, and I heard a bang. I thought a little stone from the macadam had hit the bottom of my car. A driver behind me kept sounding his horn, he was annoying me, I turned around and swore, giving him the finger, not knowing what he wanted from me. It was only when I reached the hospital parking lot that I saw that I had a burst tire. The unfortunate man had been trying to warn me, and I insulted him! I don't know how to change a tire. I called a towing firm," I said. He's changing the wheel. He doesn't say anything.

And later, in a restaurant, he refuses to eat. "What's wrong?"

"While I was changing the tire, I swallowed a heap of sand and now I feel sick."

I swallowed a heap of sand, you say.

It's November 1992. Sarajevo is in darkness; by the light of a paraffin lamp, I spend the whole night writing. Refugees in our own town, we were living on the ground floor of a house belonging to acquaintances who had moved away from the war to Egypt. I had arranged black-and-white photographs on the table in front of me and was describing their contents. You and Sanja were sleeping in the same room. And, I remember, our room was separated from the boiler house by a glass door. In the boiler house, in a tin drum, in peacetime there had been oil to heat the house, and now we used that space to store wood. That evening I had used a rubber hose to extract the oil from the bottom of the drum, I remember that I had suddenly sucked in a mouthful of the dark liquid and I couldn't rid myself of its taste the whole night. I used the oil to fill the old gas lamp illuminating the table where I was sitting, writing. And then it all happened. The sun came up, but the light refused to come through the windows into our room. It was already day outside, but in the room it was night. The two of you woke up and it was only then that I discovered, appalled, that everything around me was black, the photographs on the table were completely black, the covers of the books were black, my hands were black, the table was black, the duvet covering you was black, your face and Sanja's. We looked at one another, but we didn't recognize one another.

Black oily soot from the lamp had settled on everything. It was an image of pure horror. As though we'd woken up in a different world.

I remembered that distant morning, after you said *I swallowed a heap of sand and now I feel sick.*

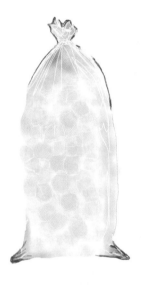

✦

At the gas station. We went in to get coffees and came out with two large bags of ice, we haven't anywhere to put them, I deposited one by my feet and set the other on my lap. My phone rang, and the voice at the other end asked: "What are you doing?"

"I'm hugging a bag of ice."

We photographed the ice as it melted. That will be a record of the specificity of the desert, an image of indisputable heat. The camera took a picture every twenty-five seconds. When they are connected later, the images will become a video that speeds up the process of melting. Where does our need to accelerate time come from? From impatience to arrive in the near future into which we have projected our trifling desires. Our need to slow time down would surely be natural. But why this strong desire to speed things up? Why are we always in a hurry to reach the future? The process of the ice melting, which looks rapid in the photographs, is an image of time that can never be restored. But perhaps there is no such thing as time?

We were protecting ourselves from the sun with a large black umbrella.

But then some loud bikers rode up to us. At first, blown up in their Harley-Davidson jackets, they looked enormous, and before they spoke to us, you said: "I'll have a word with them." That declaration of yours was something new for me. You said that because you thought you would be better at making contact with those guys, who looked threatening. Or maybe you were silencing my strong Slavic accent that might have irritated American patriots? But you haven't completely lost your accent, either, even after all these years. Or else you think that situations like this are less unusual for you than they are for me, because you spend a lot of time on the road, you sleep in the open, in the mountains, in the desert, and along the way you meet all kinds of human phenomena? Whatever it was, your judgment was obvious: on 18 April 2015, in the American desert, I was more a foreigner than you were. And in fact, I am a foreigner everywhere in the world: as soon as I leave my home, I step into a void.

The bikers asked us to let them shelter from the sun in the shade of our umbrella. The young man who spoke to us had a strong accent. And then they introduced themselves: Germans from Darmstadt, this was the second month they had been traveling through New Mexico, Arizona, and California. One had a completely white mouth, as though he had rubbed his lips with chalk, already totally dehydrated. I confessed that I worked for German television (ARD), and our recognition was followed by pure delight! It's interesting—seen from Bosnia, Germans are entirely different from us southern people. But here, on a different continent, particularly since I've been working with them, I've discovered that our similarities are great. They are close worlds, or is that just a deceptive impression by contrast with American difference? Whatever the reason, in Death Valley, we were a small misplaced tribe, under your umbrella.

✦

Darmstadt! In the autumn of 1999, during the Frankfurt
Book Fair, I stayed in the Jagdschloss Hotel in Kranichstein
near Darmstadt in the company of some cheery Balkan writers. It rained most days. It always rains in Germany. We
talked about literature and politics. On our last day, the sun
came out. And this is the only image that I remember vividly
from the few days I spent there:

The poet Ali Podrimja smoking a cigar in front of the

hotel and holding an empty wooden box of Davidoffs. A snail was making its way gradually along the concrete wall. The poet had placed the wooden lid of the box in front of the snail, expecting, I presume, that it would slowly enter the box.

I ask him: "What are you doing?"

And Podrimja says: "I'm establishing a dialogue."

We sat down on the place where the ice had melted and stayed sitting on the bare ground for a minute or two while your camera took a few photos of us. When we got back to the car, you quickly checked the photos on the camera's small screen, and we looked carefully at one of the two of us. A photograph is successful—I'm paraphrasing Barthes (*Camera Lucida*)—in which one detail, the punctum, has a magnetism that brings us back to it repeatedly. The punctum on our picture shows an obvious symmetry. You are holding your left lower arm in your right hand. That's an unconscious movement at the moment you are looking at the lens waiting for the camera automatically to take the photograph in front of it. I am also looking toward the eye of the camera and holding my lower right arm with my left hand. The same unconscious movement.

Do you remember M.? The photographer? It could have been 2002 or 2003, I took a roll of film to be developed (in those days there were shops processing film everywhere, digital photography had not yet taken over). When I collected the envelope with the printed photos a few days later, I found among them some that I first thought had been included by mistake. But they did after all show something familiar. It took a few moments for me to recognize objects from our apartment: bottles of medicine; the Sunday *Washington Post* on the floor beside the wastepaper basket; the shoes I had taken off in a hurry in the hall, and so on.

In those days, you will remember, we were friendly with M. Whenever he came to see us, he would march through all the rooms in the apartment, sniffing around before sitting down in an armchair, and then he would begin to talk. There was nothing aggressive in this, on the contrary. He used to work as a photographer for *Time* magazine, traveling through war zones: Lebanon, El Salvador, and Nicaragua. His war experiences were turned into screenplays, and one film is about the last days of Somoza's rule. A bad film, but there was one very strong scene in it: after the guerrilla leader had been killed, the news of his death spread like wildfire, and out of fear of the loss of morale and potential defeatism, the photographer was asked to photograph the dead man so that he looked alive. And a picture was taken with the newspaper of the day on the desk in front of the dead leader with his eyes open, which was published the following day on the front page of the same paper to confirm that he was still alive. Why does that scene appeal to me? Because it contains the ultimate power of photography and because no other medium is capable of bringing someone "back to life."

As he toured our rooms, M. used my camera to take pictures of everything that his eye found interesting. If I'd been asked, I'd never have taken those photos, but it's true that they told me a lot. It's interesting to discover how others see us. It's interesting to see one's own world through someone else's eyes, even when they show you a newspaper that you know for certain you leafed through but from which you can no longer recall a single article.

✦

The temperatures are so high that nothing living can inhabit this part of the desert. There are no snakes or scorpions. And then I remembered. Sometime around the beginning of the war, in May and June 1992, we were living in the studio of the fine-art group Zvono, "The Bell," with the painter Sead Čizmić, the photographer Kemal Hadžić, and their wives. There were a lot of glass walls there, a fairly risky place to live, but in the building next door there was a nuclear bunker, so we took shelter there on the days when shells were raining down on our district. I once went with Sead up to Golobrdica, where he had a rented apartment with a wonderful open view of the city and Trebević Mountain. We stayed just long enough for him to collect the rest of the clothes they had left behind. There were already sporadic power cuts in the city, so supplies of water were kept in the bath. While Sead was collecting the things we had come for, I looked around with interest, and so came to see a drowned scorpion in the full bath. I had never seen a scorpion in Bosnia before. I scooped it into one of those round, transparent Kodak film containers, the ones with yellow lids, and took it to Harun. And he kept it for a while in the war as a toy, and then the container and the scorpion disappeared.

"You were nine then . . . Do you remember that little Kodak film box?"

And he said: "Vaguely."

✦

Furnace Creek. We are sitting in the garden of a restaurant. At the next table, the German bikers have removed their boots and socks, stripping down in the desert heat. They have been cutting up lemons in front of them and are talking loudly. And then they take the lemon slices they have sucked the juice from and start throwing them at one another. German consonants in the air around us.

Harun is frowning, because I'm slowing him down in his journey. I say: "Is there anything in the world more complicated than the father-son relationship?"

We both have frequent attacks of melancholy. Our gloom is a consequence of the war. Or else, in my case, the war deepened that emotion, for melancholy was not unknown to me since my earliest childhood. And when I think of my first experiences of unbearable desolation, I see an image of the autumnal dissipation of the world, an October forest smelling of decay. I rarely write about my childhood, as though I were running away from it. If so, I'm running away from an October forest. Your childhood was different. You acquired the habit of going into the mountains quite young, in the red cabin of the Sarajevo cable car to Trebević, and then on up, along goat tracks, to the top. You memorized the rocks, tree trunks, and abandoned bunkers left over from the First World War. I would like to know how far back your memory stretches, my son.

Today I ask you whether you remember the cable car to Trebević.

And you say: "I remember my childhood in 3D, down to the smallest detail!"

But when I remind you of an event from the war, your memory becomes unreliable and vague. You suppress the war into oblivion.

A man at the next table had been listening in to our conversation, looking at me warily. That's nothing new, people around us display increasing aversion when they hear a conversation in an unfamiliar language. Over the course of the last twenty years that I've lived here, I've been able to monitor the way America has been closing up, screening itself from the outside world. It used not to be like this. When people heard a foreign language on the subway, at the airport, or like this, in a restaurant, it would arouse their curiosity, not aversion, certainly not fear. Twenty years is a long time, people pass on and worlds change. Foreigners are no longer welcome here. And, as I say, the man at the next table was looking at me awkwardly, surprised by the foreign language I was speaking.

But then there was a sudden reversal. A smiling young man in a white Armani shirt came up to our table and introduced himself: "Hi, I'm David from Murska Sobota. I was so happy when I heard you speaking our language." Then we began to talk; he said he had landed in Mexico City a month before, he was traveling from south to north, in a few days he would be flying out of San Francisco back to Slovenia. David had said he was happy to hear us speaking "our language." That language of ours was one of those spoken in Yugoslavia. But that country had long since fallen apart. In our shared country, David's language, Slovene, had also been "ours." Once, long ago, there was a world in which we called different languages "ours."

Whenever I'm in the company of strangers and speak in a way that reveals my Slav accent, the question follows: "Where are you from?" I always reply politely. It's very important to me that I say exactly where I'm from, and explain where that place is in case the person I'm talking to has never heard of my country ("in Europe, near Italy"). I suppose that's a need in me to feel accepted for what I am. Furthermore, I have a belief in the importance of conversation, something sacrosanct that comes from a conviction that there is beauty in our remaining in the memory of strangers, particularly when we first meet, knowing we'll never see them again. Showing one's true identity means showing myself the way I really am; I want to be sincere. But what does *sincerity* mean? People gladly engage in conversation not out of mere curiosity, but from caution. They aren't interested in who you are, they want confirmation that you're normal and don't represent a threat. That's the sincerity in you that interests them. They're afraid.

✦

I found a fallen eyelash under your lower left eyelid and picked it up, holding it between my fingers, but you were tired and refused to imagine a wish and didn't want to blow at my fingers. We developed this ritual in your earliest childhood: whenever we found a fallen eyelash, one of the two of us would hold it tightly between our thumb and forefinger, and then we would each blow—three times, taking it in turns, our eyes closed, each imagining a wish. Then we would choose, and if you guessed the finger the lash had stuck to, you had the right to have your wish come true. The lash would be carefully tucked under your shirt collar or pajamas, beside your heart so as not to be lost, to be close to you, so that your dream could come true. Those were the rules. But if you guessed wrong, then the lash would be mine and slipped inside my shirt to serve my wish. I ask: "Do you remember any of your wishes? And if you do, did any of them ever come true?"

And now, when it no longer matters, I can confess: I, too, had my dreams.

My wishes weren't big, but still none of them came to anything. I longed for a small window from which one could see blue water. I imagined that in my fifties I would live a peaceful life, with time freed up just for writing. I wanted a small shady café where I would meet with friends on a Saturday or Sunday morning to gossip about our past. But I ended up as a prisoner on a vast continent, alone, without people to talk to. A foreigner. And I have grown accustomed to this solitude, I have accepted it as payback for the sins I have committed in my life. And in exchange for my unfulfilled wishes.

To differentiate oneself from one's father? There'd always been that tension, it's probably natural in adolescence for a son to compare himself to his father. And I remember your college admissions interview. Your interviewer came to Alexandria, you met at the Starbucks at the end of King Street, beside the river. It was early summer, a lovely day, at the end of the garden the two of you were sitting at a table, I was at another. The distance between us was not great, so I could hear your conversation, not all of it, but I strained to hear as much as I could, and then came the moment when you said to that stranger: "My father is a writer and I want to distance myself from his interests, I want the two of us to be different and I'm not interested in literature!" I think I understood your reasons then, as I understand them now. The difference is that then your announcement ("I'm not interested in literature!") hurt me, but now I remember it all with a certain pleasure and sympathy for the you who perhaps didn't yet know what you wanted, but you evidently knew what you didn't want.

I was working in the Reuters Washington office, and Harun's student film had been quite a success; invited for an interview, he arrived early and so came in to see me in the video archive. I asked him whether he had anything against my being present at the conversation, and he said no, on the contrary. I listened with interest as he answered questions about his past. And, since his student film was concerned with war, there was inevitably a question about the siege of Sarajevo. And then he said: "All I wanted was to get out of the city, but, when asked about it, my father would always say 'No, no, I don't want to go, I refuse to allow them to drive me out of my home!'" That was the first time we had talked about the war so openly, and the conversation took place through an intermediary, Harun was replying to a journalist's question, but his answer was intended for me.

What does he think of me? He never showed any open liking for my choices. I never heard him endorse them or praise me for anything. Apart from once. While he was studying in Los Angeles, I traveled there for a reading, in a place called Villa Aurora, famous for having been an exile refuge for German writers and philosophers—Brecht, Mann, Adorno, and others—during the Second World War, and the house contains mementos of those few important years. In the days that I spent there, there were a couple of German artists living there, and a journalist, a Kurd who—people said—would have been arrested if he returned to Turkey. In the evening, I did my reading, the audience was unusual, mostly older people, escaping from the tedium of their afternoons, and my words didn't reach them. But I enjoyed the reading, above all because I had impressed Harun. He was with his new girlfriend. And afterward, in conversation with our hosts, over a glass of wine, I heard him compliment me for the first time ever, he said authoritatively: "Sem is very perceptive!" (And, yes, from his first spoken words, he had always called me by my name; all these years I had been Sem for him, except when, transferring to English, to be understood by the people he was talking to, he began to follow a more formal usage, and at times, when he was speaking with his American acquaintances, he referred to me as *my dad*.)

On the other hand, he never displayed hostility toward my choices. He couldn't identify with literature, especially poetry, which he read only reluctantly. Only later did he begin to read Rumi, indicating a tendency toward mysticism, although he made a clear barrier between himself and religion very early on. I had once tried to get him to "open up," to discover what he really thought about poetry. He resisted, but he confessed that the people he met, ever since secondary school, particularly those at college, were "frightened of poetry!" I think he said that as a compliment to poetry, its

seriousness. In his value system, everything that was not accepted by the masses was good.

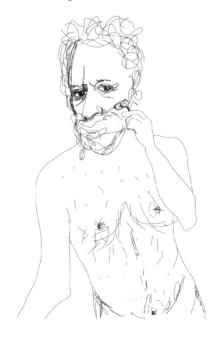

✦

There was a black pickup parked in a rest stop beside the
road, and in the shadow of the steering wheel a man stripped
to the waist was shaving blind, with no mirror.

As long as we've been on the road, I've been letting my
beard grow.

Throughout the war, for the almost four years the siege of
Sarajevo lasted, I shaved with just one razor blade.

✦

Our clothes are dusty, there's red sand on our shoes, the car is dusty, and the windshield is greasy and dirty so that one can hardly see out of it. ("It's the tiny insects that get stuck to the glass as you drive. I keep cleaning them off and they keep coming back.") Thousands of barely visible insects perishing before the driver's eyes; their microscopic deaths create a consistent splotch on the glass, ceaselessly drawn by an invisible Jackson Pollock over the American road.

There's a bunch of keys swaying from his belt. I've seen this in the United States before now, on the whole with young Latino men: they hang their keys from their belts like a decoration.

Interesting. I remember that he used to drag a similar bunch of keys around with him even as a very small child, trying to open locks he happened to come across as he toddled his way about.

I'm interested in his keys, and he shows them to me one by one, until we come to the one that suddenly becomes the most important: "This is the key to the apartment in Sarajevo."

The three-year-old goes around the large parking lot in front of our building with his bunch of keys and opens car doors. Proud that he has succeeded in unlocking the trunk of a Lada; I quickly pick him up and clasp him to me to protect him from the sudden annoyance of a large man with a mustache, the car's owner . . .

He still keeps the key to our Sarajevo apartment.

Beatty, Nevada. In our motel room, I try to remember the passwords that open my internet pages, I wanted to read the emails that had reached my inboxes and reconnect with real life . . . On my home computer these pages open automatically and don't need a password. I've forgotten all of them. This is Harun's laptop, a machine that treats me like an indifferent stranger. The past with its real keys was better. It would be good today to have a bunch of keys like the one swinging from his jeans belt instead of all these passwords. It was all far easier in the twentieth century because our privacy was less wary of the public gaze, and we were more serene in our solitudes. But now in a remote desert motel, in a town called Beatty on the very border of Nevada, I stare at the computer screen. I've forgotten my password, and for a moment I feel lost, as though I don't exist. That's a brief attack of helplessness. And, since I didn't know the password, I closed the computer and felt some relief to be liberated from my daily routine. It's good to travel. I went out of the motel room onto the veranda as though I had walked out of my personal prison into freedom. I was met by a blast of hot air, it was nearly midnight.

✦

Las Vegas. The street is called Dean Martin Drive. A mechanic is changing the tire on the wheel. There's a beautiful girl with us in the waiting room, sitting in an armchair and drawing on her bare legs with a felt-tip. The two of us were commenting on her drawings. She couldn't have known that we were talking about her. When he had changed the tire, the mechanic came into the waiting room, waited for us to finish our conversation, then asked: "What language are you speaking?"

What language are we speaking? When we came here, you were young enough to adopt the rules of your new world without resistance, and for your new language to be closer to you than the one you arrived with. It was different for me, as I haven't managed to tear myself away from the past, which means that I'm a prisoner of my language. Does that mean that you and I, father and son, speak different languages?

My world is in my language, and I've never begun to write in the language of the country where I'm now living. To be truly accepted, to transform myself from a foreigner into a local, a precondition is restructuring into the new language. And that's fine. I have chosen to remain a foreigner. Once, some ten years ago, after the translation of my second book came out, an American poet explained to me, in a restaurant in Iowa, that all my problems would be solved as soon as I started writing in English. She said, very seriously, that I should just make a rough translation of my poems, she'd sort out the language, and then I could publish them as originals. She literally suggested that. I said that I didn't have any problems that needed solving. I thanked her and explained that this one language in which I wrote was enough for me, and I wouldn't want to change it. But, following my explanation, her eyes filled with tears. To be honest, her offer had offended me, but the fact that she ended up crying completely disconcerted me. I didn't know what to say, because I didn't understand the real reason for her tears. Perhaps she hadn't expected my reaction, and now her offer had been shown to be discourteous, but perhaps she was really sad to see in me a stranger who couldn't be helped? She looked at me as though she had just found out that I had a disease from which I would soon die.

About ten years ago, when he was in college, Harun went to the Slavic department to take a foreign-language exam. The foreign language in this case was his mother tongue, but from an American perspective there was no room for doubt, the local language was English and every other language was foreign. The examiner, Michael Heim, met him in his book-filled office. Harun introduced himself and asked about the possibility of taking an exam. The professor suggested that he take the exam immediately, if he felt ready. And then he went to a shelf and took down a book from which Harun was to read, to confirm his knowledge of his own language. Professor Heim put the book down on the table in front of the student and suggested that he read from the page to which he'd opened at random. And so it was. Harun began to read the text, trying to hide his smile. The professor noticed his student's unusual behavior, interrupted his reading, and asked: "The character in the story has the same name as you?" And Harun said: "Yes, but that's because this story is about me, I am the character in the story." His response astonished Professor Heim, he took the book from his hand, looked at the open page, then back at the student: "All these years, I have read a lot of books in this room, but this is the first time that I have spoken in real life to a character from a story." The book was *Sarajevo Marlboro* by Miljenko Jergović.

After we came to America, he quickly mastered the language, his new world opened up to him far more quickly and clearly than to me, he soon became a local, while I remained a foreigner. And then came generational differentiation. He stopped asking me questions, my world was as familiar to him as a book he'd read or a film he'd seen, while I began asking him questions about everything I found foreign but was part of his reality. It was as though we had changed roles overnight.

Besides, he rarely opens up, he doesn't show emotions, indeed he hides them resolutely. He is the diametric opposite of me: I immediately make all my feelings public. This makes him old-fashioned, the way Bosnian fathers used to be, and probably still are, believing that showing emotion is a sign of weakness. In that division, it was as though we had changed ages or generational places. He behaves toward me like a father, while I am a child to him. I'm more foreign here than he is. But I know that he also sees himself as foreign, from the way he reacts to the Asian tourists taking photographs of themselves beside his pickup, convinced presumably that both the vehicle and its driver are authentic locals. He laughs at that, as though it is a misunderstanding. That we are foreigners I know from the silence that sets in when a policeman stops us on the road, as we sit calmly in the truck waiting for him to speak to us.

Arizona. The question the policeman asked him after he had stopped us on the road: "How many guns do you have in the vehicle?"

This evening we looked at the photographs taken the previous day. I was surprised to find myself in the pictures, as I had not been aware I was being photographed. They are chance portraits. Harun had arranged his cameras to record the landscape in front of us for several hours, and during that time we stayed here, we chatted, stretched, looked at the sky, moved to the left or right; I forgot about the cameras around us, and that's how I happened to wander unconsciously into the space in front of their lenses and those chance portraits came into being.

In Washington it often happens on the street that I enter into the space between a person with a camera and the other person being photographed, or a group of people smiling at the camera lens, and then my picture is taken. Or else I pass behind the people taking photos of each other. I'm on my way somewhere, not thinking about what has just happened. This happens to everyone. I have many unknown people in my photographs, I don't know anything about them, I have never, until this moment, thought about those chance passersby, or about myself in other people's photos. But in fact, a small miracle has taken place: I've entered the private world of some unknown people: I'm that stranger on the edge, in the background of the photograph. They know nothing about me, they take no notice of me: they see themselves in those photos; unknown and nameless, I'm not the subject here, but rather an object, just like the façade of the building behind them or the glass shop window. Some future observer will be more curious about the bird on the shoulder of the bronze horseman in the background than about me. But, nevertheless, I still exist in all those photographs. In those pictures I will never see. In a similar but far more intensive way, we exist in other people's dreams. If those dreams could be transposed onto film, it would be interesting to see the whole, your life grown out of other people's consciousness! I would like to see myself in someone else's dream.

There are a lot of photographs from our past in which I'm holding you in my arms. And a father carrying his son in his arms is altogether a common sight. Far less frequent—and its complete opposite in emotional impact—is the image of a son carrying his father. Such as Aeneas carrying his old, weary father as they flee from burning Troy . . . I would not wish to live to a great age.

You lived in that apartment for just a few months, in the summer of 2002. Los Angeles. An apartment on two floors, in the upper one were you and your girlfriend, while the lower one was occupied by a girl about whom you didn't know much yourself, apart from her name. ("She's one of those girls who come to this city with the hope of making it into film, but if that doesn't happen they spend the best years of their lives waitressing in cheap bars and nightclubs.") After I arrived for a short visit, I went down to the lower floor for a shower. And then the girl appeared in the bathroom doorway, in a short denim skirt and T-shirt. She was smiling, she didn't ask me who I was or how I had gotten here, instead she took off her clothes and stepped naked into the shower. I was unprepared for what had happened, I already had one leg out of the bath, but she held me back in an embrace and kissed me, if it could be called a kiss. At the moment when our lips met, there was a little spark of static electricity and I covered my mouth with my hand as though physically injured by that kiss. I got out of the bath and, apologizing, picked up my things and slowly made my way to the upper floor. I was quite disconcerted. I didn't tell you anything about it of course, and I'm not sure that I would even have known how to describe properly what had happened, but I remember the unease I felt then, as though I were on the verge of incest. I still remember that girl today well enough that I could easily draw her face. I don't know why I'm telling this story now or why I remembered it. Perhaps I could have kept it quiet.

During the day, we make our way through the desert; at night he photographs the sky. Along the way, we both take pictures of the earth that catch our attention. Recording the sky is like hunting, like night fishing—he arranges his cameras and then we sit and wait for their lenses to catch a set number of pictures. That takes hours. (You're a hunter, that's now becoming quite obvious to me. Images of melting lead and making shotgun pellets in your early childhood, in northern Bosnia, filling the cartridges with tiny balls of lead, hunters' tales round the fire, that's what you remembered as essential, as your first memories to which you return . . .) Awake the whole night, we sit in the car, or stretch our arms outside, gazing at the stars, talking. When we run out of topics of conversation, we sit and each do our own thing. I draw. And last night, in the motel, I drew until almost daybreak. A photograph documents existence, although in fact it always shows something that no longer exists. A drawing is something else. It doesn't have the strength of a document, a drawing is unreliable when compared to the reality seen with one's own eyes, and so it fictionalizes my notes from our journey. And that unreliability is a good description of my journey with Harun, because over these last days my past has been dangerously mixed up with reality.

A red scarf. You belonged to the last generation of Tito's "Pioneers." Do you remember, when you started school, as part of your ceremonial uniform, you received a Partisan cap with a five-pointed star and a red scarf to be worn round the neck?

Little Pioneer! For five days now I've been watching you negotiate the roads and the desert. Tito would be proud of you!

✦

I thought that your red bandana was your photographer's uniform. Did we use the word *bandana* in Bosnia? Or were all the various kinds of scarves all called by the same common name? I don't remember. I've begun to forget my own language. Did we use the word *fedora*, or was all headwear of that kind just called a *hat*?

It's interesting, this spring a brown fedora appeared on our coat stand, bought many years ago, but I had never stepped outside the house wearing it. I should also say that I had not written anything for months and was fairly despondent as a result. And two Saturdays ago, as soon as I woke up, in my pajamas, on my way to my desk I picked up the hat and put it on, just to see what it looked like on my head. I can say that this little change pleased me. Every day now I go to my desk in my pajamas with the hat on my head, that's now my working uniform, because I started writing again when I was wearing it. It's a purely theatrical effect: once I had put the hat on my head, I entered into a role. Like a character, like someone else, I began to write unimpeded, perhaps because it's easier to express one's opinions in someone else's name; in other words, with the fedora on my head, I freed myself of the responsibility of being "me." That "I" is the source of my despondency, it's my daily terrorist.

But you think differently: "I cover my hair with a scarf so

it doesn't get in my way when I'm taking photographs. Or I soak the scarf in water to cool me in the desert."

Our desert soundtrack: "Blood Like Lemonade," Morcheeba—"Scott & Zelda," Tiny Victories—"New Dawn Fades," Moby—"Blackout," Hybrid—"Chord Sounds," Moby—"Beachcoma," Hybrid—"The Ghost Inside," Broken Bells.

Zagreb, November 1995–January 1996. You escape obsessively into video games. Super Mario's musical phrase, repeated ad infinitum, was our Croatian refugee soundtrack.

What did you say this town is called? Above the front doors of the houses in the main street, lights are on all day long.

It was already pitch dark, we were driving toward an abandoned mining town (Rhyolite), when a wild rabbit leaped out onto the road in front of us, disappearing under the moving car. Crazy bunny! But there was no sound, nothing had happened. We stopped and looked into the darkness beside the road—"I didn't kill it."

"No, you didn't."

Last autumn, we were driving after midnight through Shenandoah Valley, when out of the fog in front of us a group of alarmed deer—stags, does, and their young, hundreds of them—crossed from the left to the right side of the road, it must have been the time of year for them to migrate, and we had to drive very slowly, and we were in a hurry to get home. Fog and fear of blood and damp, warm fur.

What am I doing? I'm describing events that you witnessed on this journey, or you were present in them, in the recent or more distant past. But that's all right. It's not wrong to describe for another something he can see for himself. What else do sports commentators do in the course of a broadcast match? What they describe can be irritating for the spectators watching it. But I'm doing this because I'm interested now above all in events where we were both present, I'm interested in images from our shared memory. I came here with the intention that we should compare those memories, so that I would discover something about my forgetfulness. And have I discovered anything? No. In fact I've found that you suppress certain memories (above all of the war). Your reasons are understandable. I envy you that, because my most intense memories are of events I would gladly forget. Remembering and forgetting stand side by side, they're made of the same substance. "Forgetting is the absent brother of Remembering," says Cees Nooteboom.

An abandoned mining town on the edge of the desert. After the miners left, artists lived here for a while. Then they, too, left, while their sculptures remained. Art and ruins.

When nature takes them over, when ivy covers the walls, when a pine tree starts to grow through a roof—abandoned houses have an unexpected beauty . . . But abandoned places are unprotected and there are always those who come to wreak havoc and destroy with impunity.

"That fine house," you say, "the one I photographed last month, has burned down."

"What happened?"

"Vandals set fire to it . . ."

I understand your liking for abandoned places. A photograph of a starry sky above unpopulated houses has a magnetic beauty. But when destructiveness overwhelms that state of abandonment and absence, such a place loses all its appeal. We roamed with flashlights through the derelict town, looking for subjects suitable for the cameras. But we found nothing. It's not worth taking pictures here, we'll have to wait for nature's power once again to cover over the traces of human presence.

You gaze at the sky through your camera lens, while I can just make out in the darkness in front of me the ruined wall of a building, and I think of Fred, a fireman who turned up in Sarajevo during the war. He carried out various humanitarian tasks, he was useful, he used to leave the city, travel back to America, and keep coming back to our besieged city. After Sarajevo, in 1995, he went to Chechnya, and all trace of him was lost. He vanished. And in the eighties, somewhere in Latin America, he had fallen asleep, weary, in a hotel. In the morning he woke, looked out the window, and saw destroyed buildings as far as the eye could see. He opened his door and realized that he was on the edge of an abyss, because the corridor and stairs had collapsed. He had slept through an earthquake that had turned the whole town into a ruin. It had vanished.

✦

From our hotel room I see airport lights, planes like fireflies take off and land.

"What airport is that?" I ask.

"Military! Beyond the runway is Area 51."

I stand at the window and watch. For more than thirty years, on various continents, we have lived within reach of an airport. The apartment where I now live is some two hundred yards as the crow flies from the runway of a Washington airport (DCA). On my way to work, I like to stop in there and have a morning coffee surrounded by travelers, I find their passenger tension soothing, and perhaps I'm also encouraging myself with the thought that one morning instead of carrying on to work, I'll buy a ticket and fly off out of my life. Our first airport was the one in Sarajevo. We moved there in the early 1980s. There was a restaurant called Kula near the eastern end of the runway. It was an unusual restaurant, as it was staffed by prisoners. On the whole, petty criminals, or at least that was the word in public, although I always suspected that there were murderers among them. Beside the restaurant building there was a tidily maintained plot where the prisoners tended vegetables, fruit, and domestic animals . . . We went there from time to time. And once, in the early summer, instead of a leisurely stroll to the restaurant, we went by a roundabout route and then a shortcut across a field of tall grasses. When we reached the restaurant garden Sanja's face was swollen and red, her breathing difficult—we didn't know what had happened to begin with, but we were to discover in the course of the day in the emergency room that she had had a violent allergic attack. For the following seven or eight years, she was seriously ill, but she coped bravely with her allergy. When the siege of Sarajevo began, at the end of April 1992, we moved to within reach of the hospital, because of her illness, so as to be closer to the doctors. But, interestingly, during the war her allergy almost completely disappeared and she had almost no need for medication. My acquaintance and colleague the poet Radovan Karadžić turned the restaurant into a concentration camp. Many of my friends were among the prisoners there. On the whole good people. In the world there is a rule that great suffering happens to the good people. Then, during the siege, I left the city several times through a tunnel under the runway, and came back, and in the end I left, crossing that same runway, perhaps forever.

"Area 51, you say?"

An elderly couple, with walking sticks, lean on each other as they walk. They got out of their car at a gas station, and, dependent on each other in their mutual support, they went inside to buy a sack of ice. Ice is something you can't do without in the desert. But what are such old people doing in the desert at the very end of their lives? Of all places in the world? A desert? With their sticks, leaning on each other, they inch forward together, step by step.

I'm reading in the desert. I bought this book after I heard that it contained a story by an acquaintance of mine. It's a book of very short stories, which they call here *flash fiction* because of their striking brevity. The contents state that the story is on page 43. But when I opened the book, the story was not there, my acquaintance was not in the book, only in the table of contents. There is no page 43 in the book, page 42 continues on page 44 and so on. I wanted to exchange my copy of the book (with the error) for a correct one, but in the bookshop it turned out that there was no page 43 in any copies of the book. A book with a vanished story, an anthology with a vanished author.

But everything I read in the desert lacks weight. The desert silence drowns out our sentences. And I think about the fact that our writing was flawed, because we were in a hurry to transpose into words an event in which Something happened, whereas over and over again we should have been describing a state in which Nothing happens.

At the beginning of the 1990s, I had a small bookshop in the Sarajevo Society of Writers, beside the stairs leading to the upper floor and the garden behind the building. I sometimes went there with you, when you were seven or eight, your interest in the space and the people who gathered there didn't last long and you would begin to get bored. If my friend Dario happened to be in the building, he would take you to the video shop in Kralj Tomislav Street and you would rent some videocassettes. You would stay in his apartment near the military hospital, watching films, while he came back to keep me company in the bookshop. Later, in the war, the video shop ceased to exist, an acquaintance of ours opened a restaurant on the premises, a very attractive and agreeable place, with old sofas and comfortable armchairs. There were some forgotten videocassettes there, and they were used as decorations in the restaurant. Someone else occupied Dario's apartment during the war, and he tried for years to get back into his room. When he finally succeeded, he died. The bookshop, too, ceased to exist. In the early summer of 1992, I went there to see what state the books were in, but the writers who were supposedly taking care of the building had thrown them out, into the rain. My books in the rain.

Do you remember, once we were going to a soccer field behind your secondary school in Falls Church and you asked me to let us out of the car in the big parking lot, just so that you could show me the place where an angry, armed high school pupil had killed a girl from your class? We found a few wilted flowers on the spot. We stood there, you spoke softly, still unsettled by the event, you raised your arm and pointed toward the school building in front of us and said: "I was at that window, and I saw everything."

My PTSD, and your PTSD.

We are two bodies filled with traumas that were never

appropriately treated. I feel guilty for not having taken you out of Sarajevo during the war. That's why I've been indulging you all these years, fulfilling your wishes and protecting you. And I know that this doesn't do you any good: all these years I have been weighing you down with care and supervision, I'm a burden that slows you down and from which you would, probably, gladly free yourself, but nevertheless you put up with me. My additional problem is the way in which your PTSD manifests itself. You are attracted to danger, and that's a consequence of the war, adrenaline dependency. That's why you spend whole nights in empty spaces, under the stars, meeting people there who have their own reasons for insomnia. Everyone here is armed. The world is a dangerous place. I, too, am a frightened man. Perhaps you should have a dog to be near you on these nights and look after you. A German shepherd? A husky would suit you, one with blue eyes. Two wolves in the desert! I'll bring you a puppy to grow up beside you. And I'll buy a bandana, which you could tie around his neck. Maybe blue? To go with his eyes . . .

It was still light when we reached Phoenix, three hours before my flight; we had enough time to go back once more to "our" apartment. The sun was going down, so the evening light above the city was orange. In the parking lot in front of the complex, we found a free space. We went through the narrow door into the courtyard between the six buildings, linked by iron fences. The light of the setting sun no longer penetrated here, and suddenly it was dusk; lamps were being lit in the windows of the ground-floor apartments, and as we walked I glanced into the rooms in the hope of possibly seeing a familiar face. At a stone table beside the empty swimming pool a girl was sitting in the company of three men who paid no attention to us. She was very young, and I thought that at the time when we lived here she hadn't yet been born. The empty beer bottles and the blue canvas chair faded in the sun were still beside the door of our apartment. The windows were dark, either there was no one there or the tenant had fallen asleep. I sat down on the canvas chair. "There's no point in taking your photograph now," said Harun. "The light's not good enough." I sat on the canvas chair, which I may have brought here twenty years earlier, looking at the empty bottles of Miller Lite beer, which I might have left behind, and waited for something to happen. It couldn't be that I'd come back and this place had no response to my return. I sat on the canvas chair after a week spent on the road, after troubled dreams in cheap motels and deserts under the starry sky. And I had felt more or less at home everywhere, apart from here, at the address 1601 Camelback Road, no. 201! Here I am most foreign. And now I can calmly forget everything.

"Let's go!" says Harun.

"Just one more minute," I say. And then we wait for that minute to pass.

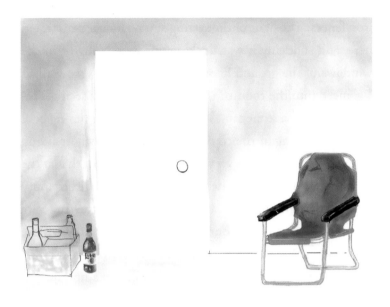

✦

But what is most important always remains unsaid! We parted in haste, a quick hug, meager words still hovered in the air, your red pickup had already disappeared among the other vehicles in the dusk, and I wanted to say:

"Son, I came finally to free you of myself! There, you're free, go off into your desert!"

Son,

You're on your way to your home, and I'm at the airport and will soon be on the plane. And the moment I found an empty table in the airport café, I saw a sparrow flying over the large waiting area opposite and I thought of Tomaž Šalamun. A poet, he had the habit, whenever he came to America on his writer's business, of calling from those hotels within reach of the airport, after his flight had been canceled, or he would simply call from an airport café like this one, and then we would chat while he waited for his flight. Ever since I've lived here, my most important contacts with friends have been carried out like that. Over the telephone. On one occasion, his flight from Denver was canceled because of heavy snow; I said that I was familiar with the boredom that engulfs one at airports, but that there is no greater loneliness than that of hotel rooms within reach of the airport, while we wait for the next day's flight; he disagreed, because that was not the case with him, in a plane or at an airport or in an airport hotel he was never bored. And he said then: "Even when I'm not particularly in the mood for writing, I write a few poems on the plane." Whenever I'm at an airport, I search for Šalamun's password that would liberate me of my solitude. And I always look carefully around me until I catch sight of a sparrow. In every airport there is a sparrow fluttering its wings anxiously under the building's glass cupolas. The official airport sparrow.

There. Our journey was good. Now I know that the two of us are very much alone. Two solitudes. When we first arrived in this city, you were thirteen, I was thirty-five, now you are thirty-three and the contemporary of the me of twenty years ago. Time melts more quickly than ice in the desert.

In fact, time is not the issue, since I passed fifty, I know that everyone dies young. The question is: What will you make of your solitude? Look after yourself, drive carefully, and read clever books. Lock the house when you go out, and always take a sweater with you, the weather can change abruptly.

> The clouds were the color of oil, Harun
> > wanted to take
> a few photographs of the sky. And then it
> > began to rain.
> We took shelter in a café, the one by the
> > Russian shop
> where we buy food from Slavic lands.
> We scurried in and sat down at the only free
> > table.
> Now bent over a camera we look
> at the pictures you've taken, surprised by the
> > look of the clouds
> that we'd seen in reality a couple of
> > minutes ago.
> There's a sullen-looking type at the next
> > table.
> I didn't notice him when we came in,
> I pay attention when he asks: "Russians?"
> And then he says: "Go back to Russia!"

He has *The Washington Post* on his lap,
who knows what he's been reading there
    today
that makes our Slavic accent so irritating
that he lost control and said: "Go back to
    Russia!"

I was wounded and angry. When our eyes
    met, he drew his head
into his shoulders and sank more deeply
    into the leather armchair.

Only then do I see the woman sitting
    beside him.
She says: "Let's go home."
He says: "We can't, it's raining."
She says: "So what? We'll run to the car."

The two of them live together. I paid
    attention to her,
because it was easy to recognize her Russian
    accent when she spoke.

They soon left, but when they were already
    at the door,

he turned back to tell me once again: "Go
    back to Russia!"
She turned to us with an apologetic look.
Then they started to run. And when they
    reached the other side of the road,
They could no longer be seen for the rain.

SNOWFLAKE

Love is a form of forgetting.
—RICHARD HELL

When they carried her out of our apartment into the rainy day, she was in pain and barefoot, so she turned and told me to bring her "some shoes." I picked up the first ones I found. I drove behind the ambulance in which she was traveling toward the hospital, glancing from time to time at those white tennis shoes on the passenger seat. Rain and the monotonous sound of the wipers. Canvas tennis shoes are not for a rainy day. Sanja was in the red vehicle in front of me, her shoes were following her.

In the hospital, two doctors asked her synchronized questions and she answered. Questions about her allergy, about her medical history, she answered with wide-open eyes in the face of the authority of the two men in their white coats, as though she were taking an exam. And then one asked: "Do you smoke?"

"Yes," she said, "but only two or three cigarettes a day."

She's no good at lying, in situations like this she will sincerely confess everything. When I heard her answer the doctor's question, I thought that may well have been the case: at work she probably smoked two or three cigarettes, but she'd kept it from me, because she was very anxious not to revive my desire for tobacco (and in the past I had been pretty dependent). After my heart attack, five years ago, she, too, stopped smoking, out of solidarity, or at least she didn't light a cigarette in my presence. She had smoked "two or three cigarettes a day" all her life, and it had never become a real addiction.

More than twenty-four hours had passed since that conversation with the doctors, and now it had become clear why she had said she was a smoker: she had suffered a stroke and one of the consequences was forgetting. The stroke had damaged her so-called short-term memory so that she'd forgotten the last three years when she no longer went out onto the balcony to smoke.

She looks at her arm, which she can only move with difficulty, and asks: "What's happened to me, Sem?"

"Yesterday," I say, "I was making coffee, you'd gone to the

bathroom, everything was all right, it was raining. As I was pouring water into the machine, I heard a cry from the bathroom, I thought you'd fallen, but that wasn't it, your arm was hurting, you said it was tingling and you couldn't feel your fingers. You didn't want us to call an ambulance, but you weren't getting any better, so I did call. They came, and after a quick examination, decided to take you to hospital. I drove behind the red ambulance and when I reached the hospital, you were already in bed, a nurse was giving you morphine, you were already having a transfusion, then they took you away, with your bed, to a different room where they did a CT scan. It had turned out that you were very anemic, so they sent you to the oncology department, as they thought you had cancer. The CT showed that you had a clot in an artery near your left shoulder, and they said it had caused a stroke, or rather a series of mini strokes in the peripheral microvascular tips on the left side of your brain. And now, because you're anemic, they don't know how to treat you. A stroke is treated with blood thinners, but the reason for your anemia is potentially an internal bleed. So now, if they put you on thinners, it would exacerbate the bleed and that would be a serious problem . . ."

She looks at me anxiously, but she has already forgotten what she asked me, and has already forgotten my reply, and now she asks again: "What has happened to me?"

✦

The first night in the hospital. She sleeps and wakes in short bursts, her sleep is shallow. She wakes up, looks at me with an expression of disappointment on her face and asks:

"Is Daddy angry with me?"

"Are you asking whether your father is angry?"

"Yes, he's angry with me and that's why he's not coming home . . ."

"Listen," I say, "your father died four or five years ago."

She thought for a while, it seemed she had remembered, then she put her head on the pillow again and went back to sleep. What had actually happened? She'd woken up in her hospital bed as a little girl of five. That was a time capsule, a trauma of fifty years earlier and now it was alive in her: her father wasn't coming home because he was angry with her. Oh, my little frightened girl!

Her father. I never met him, although we lived in the same town for sixteen long years. He never tried to contact his daughter, nor did he ever show any kind of interest in her. That was all important to me, of course, but I didn't ask, I left it up to her to talk about it, or not. And she rarely mentioned him. So I know nothing about him, apart from her incidental, sparse anecdotes. One was from her early childhood. Somewhere near the coast, they had a caravan. During the night he came with an unknown woman, woke his daughter, and took her outside, forcing her to spend the night in the rain. A little girl at night, in the rain. Nothing connects me to him, apart from the fact that he marked my life indirectly, influenced it, and altered my personality over time. Through his relationship with his daughter, he formed her hostility toward the whole male species. We have lived together for thirty years, and all that time she has been wary of me. I never saw him, but I bear that man as my personal burden. I'm tired of him. And I'm used to him. The other image is connected with Libya. Her memory of Africa, where she lived on the sensitive cusp between childhood and youth was quite bright and consoling. She would often say: "I'd like to go back to Africa." That was where she spent her last summer with both her parents. Remembering Libya, she would always mention her father: "He immediately felt at home there, he quickly learned Arabic, and began to make friends with the local people." Then she'd talk indifferently, as though describing a stranger. Later, when he left, she didn't miss him. We're now on the verge of old age, but one doesn't stop being a child at fifty. All these years, she hasn't missed him, that concrete man, but a father, one who ought by biological imperative to be on her side, when a daughter needs protection and security.

She woke up a little while ago as a little five-year-old girl who had blamed herself fifty years earlier because her daddy hadn't come home for days.

I keep finding her white tennis shoes in different places. Maybe the nurses move them? I haven't moved them. Or else they move around the ward on their own, impatient to get out of here as soon as possible. Yesterday, with her bag and white tennis shoes, I came through the transparent hospital door that opens in a circle, asked directions to the emergency room, where she'd been taken, intending to wait for the medication that would cure the pain in her arm, and then help her to tie the laces on her white tennis shoes, hold her hand as we crossed the parking lot to our car, and we'd drive home slowly, return to our everyday concerns, finish the tasks we'd begun in the kitchen: turn on the coffee machine, into which I had already poured water, spooned the coffee . . . But that wouldn't happen, the doctors would meet us with bad news, she'd be settled into the oncology ward, and I'd stay beside her all night, like a loyal dog.

It all happened too fast. The doctors stated that, in all probability, she had cancer. I held her hand while she slept, she clasped mine tightly, because she was dreaming about something. And I thought, She isn't dying, because dying people no longer dream! A ridiculous thought, but I held on to her till the morning, because there was no one there who could console me. The warmth of her hand and her whole sleeping body was the only acceptable reality for me.

All my life I have borne the burden of my meaningless name. But I came to terms with that early on, convinced it was after all just a name, that it didn't matter what a boat was called, just that it could sail, and that we fill the being bearing our name with the glow of our being. It was a consoling thought. It's only today, in my fifty-sixth year, that I have completely accepted and identified with my name. This is why. The doctor asks her: "What year is this? Which month? Where are we now?" She looks at him and there's no reply, she has forgotten the year and the month and the place. Then the doctor points at me, sitting beside her bed, "And who is this man?" For a moment she settled her gaze, she appeared to be looking right through me, and I felt a chill run through my whole body. And I thought: She's forgotten me. But then her face experienced a total transformation, she looked at me as though she had saved me from nonexistence, or as though she had just given birth to me, and with an expression of the purest love she said: "Semezdin, my Semezdin." And that was the moment when my name filled with meaning. I was *her Semezdin*. That is my love story, and my whole life.

All of a sudden, bodies in a hospital start to become distorted. The nurse who injects her with morphine looks pear-shaped. Her head is minuscule in comparison with the rest of her body. It's probably due to some inner optic problem of mine, which recurs whenever I find myself in a hospital. That is, I see human bodies as defective and incomplete. Perhaps because in a hospital a body is transformed from a subject into an object. But as soon as I get outside, my gaze becomes normal and I see people the way they, presumably, are. So a hospital becomes in my eyes like a crooked mirror, which distorts bodies. And then it seems to me that it's the presence of people that makes this world imperfect, when it's otherwise beautiful and amazing!

H. Gallasch, my friend from work, brought us food from an Italian restaurant and briefly took me outside the hospital to breathe in some fresh air. Through the big circular door we went slowly out into the rain. Everything in the hospital had slowed down, adapted to the movements of the patient. Time slowed down as well. From our ward, you had to pass through a labyrinth of corridors to come out into the rain. "It's just as well you aren't a smoker," said H. "Otherwise you'd be popping in and out for a smoke." I didn't stay long outside, it was a cold April day, we said goodbye and I went back inside through the round door that revolved so slowly. I glanced at the paper sack of food in my hand and saw an image of Venice showing a palace and bridge with a gondola passing under it, and suddenly the revolving door became a time capsule.

Venice. The night before last, I was reading an essay about Venice by Sergio Pitol, his first encounter with the town, which he saw through a fog because he had lost his glasses somewhere on the way. I read that two nights ago, which now seems like the distant past, or some other life. And while I was reading, I could smell cement, because a few hours earlier, at work, my friend Santiago Chillari had been showing me photographs of the inside of an old building beside one of the Venetian canals, which he and his family are restoring with the intention of turning it into a hotel; the photos were of workmen scraping the walls, stripping off the old paint, with building materials, sacks of cement around them on the floor . . . After reading this piece about Venice, I wrote one about Aleš Debeljak, my friend who died tragically two months ago, I thought about him and jotted down memories of our encounters. We used to meet often, speak on the phone, and exchange emails. We got to know each other in the early 1980s, but it seems to me that our contact became pure friendship only last year: in October, at a literary conference in Richmond, for a few days we shared a common balcony in our hotel and chewed over our two pasts in lengthy conversations. I went through my email inbox to find his last sentence to me. His last message ended with the announcement: "This evening I'm taking our dog on our regular walk beside the Venice-Budapest train-line." A poet! So a whole cultural space was transformed into the boundaries of a "regular" evening stroll.

The door described a complete circle, and I stepped back, into the hospital . . .

In the morning, as I was washing my face, I spotted in the mirror some white strands of hair on my forehead. Only two days have passed since we got here, and I'm already going gray.

When the nurse comes into the ward to give her an injection, Sanja says, "You smell nice," to please her, to establish human contact with a small compliment before the pain.

Otherwise I think there's something deeply problematic about the way treatment is managed in a hospital. Every ten minutes people come to check her name and date of birth; to scan the bar code on the plastic armband around her right wrist; to take her pulse, blood pressure, temperature; to take blood samples, knock her knee with a rubber hammer . . . It's torture by lack of sleep, and it could all be done in a slower rhythm, so that the patients have time to catch their breath, to fall asleep, to have a minimal amount of rest, at least during the night. A hospital ward is a torture chamber. I think hospitals ought to sign the Geneva Convention and stick rigorously to the rules.

I put my T-shirts on her, because they're bigger and more comfortable than hers. I've got one here that's the color of the September sky in Sarajevo on a sunny, cloudless day. That's the one she likes best.

It's three in the morning now. Through the high hospital window I count the planes descending from the night sky to the airport, the lights from their windows merging with the oc-casional lights from the windows of houses in Arlington. She opened her eyes briefly, glanced at me, then turned onto her other side and went on hovering between sleep and waking. She glanced at me, but I'm not convinced she knew who I was.

It's three in the morning. I have always liked her early wakings. When I used to write at night, it sometimes hap-pened that I woke her because I would forget to move the kettle off the heat before it whistled. So I might wake her at three in the morning and she was always cheerful, ready to joke. There she is in the doorway, she looks at me, shakes her head, and says: "You're fifty years old and still writing ditties!" And once, woken like that, still half asleep, she said: "The Chinese believe that dragons like the smell of copper." Dawn is her time of day. That's why I remember many of her morning sentences. Showered, her hair wet, ready for work, she would spread out her arms and ask: "Is someone going to tell me I'm beautiful?"

She has forgotten everything. She asks: "How old am I?" Whatever number I tell her, she'll believe it. So I ask her her date of birth, because she has to answer that question every five minutes for one of the hospital staff.

"September 17, 1960!"

And I say: "Now it's 2016. Can you work out how much time has passed between 1960 and 2016?"

She closes her eyes and counts. Then she looks up and says, "I can't be that old!"

Befuddled by the painkillers, she easily drifts into sleep and even more easily wakes from it. She woke briefly and said anxiously that she kept sleeping and she ought to get up, because she'd be late for an exam at the university. And then I didn't have the heart to tell her that our student youth is far behind us, in a past that would be best forgotten for our own good, in a state that no longer officially exists, in a world that is no more.

I went back to our apartment to bring some essential things that we'll need in the hospital, some clothes, toothpaste and a toothbrush, some fruit, in case she gets hungry. I picked up the mail from our mailbox. On the way to the apartment I opened a package in which there was a book, I leafed through it briefly and read a sentence from the first paragraph: "All our problems are a consequence of our not being prepared to stay inside." I walked along the corridor through which she had gone in the opposite direction the day before yesterday. Our lengthy corridor. From the elevator to our door the distance is the length of two football fields. Once, weary, I stood at our apartment door, having set off on an urgent errand in town, but when I looked along the lengthy corridor, I lost the will, I couldn't face the long walk to the elevator, so I turned around and closed the door behind me.

✦

It was less than two days since I'd been in the apartment, but when I went in memories had me reeling, first of the previous morning, and then of all the days spent here, because every object in the apartment reminded me of the motion of her hand putting it in that place. I took a shower and changed. On the computer I tried to find out what household maintenance tasks needed attending to. I know nothing about that, she did it all. And my system soon collapsed in the face of all those passwords! I'd now need to reconstruct our reality from scratch, or would it be better to wait for Sanja to remember everything? I stood in the kitchen thinking about Saturday morning, before she complained about a pain in her arm. I had been about to make coffee for the two of us, I had poured the water into the machine, spooned finely ground coffee into the filter, all I had to do was to press the button on the coffee machine. I did that now, and the sound of bubbling water drove the silence out of our room. I made coffee for two. I poured mine into a glass cup, but what to do with hers? And I don't know how to emerge from that Saturday morning. I want to freeze the time in my memory, to keep us there in the room, to prolong for as long as possible the peace in which two people are getting ready to drink their morning coffee. I want to stop everything in the state before her stroke, before the pain. We won't leave the house!

✦

I'll try again to describe that reaction that filled me with anxiety. When I entered our apartment, I glanced at the familiar objects around me, thinking at the same moment that all those objects were imprinted with the movement of Sanja's hand. She had put each object in its place and it was the movement of her hand that had maintained those objects' sheen. That thought was dangerous because I was, unconsciously, seeing a world without her, just the movement of her hand. That's what brought on this anxiety, the swelling around my heart.

Her invisible veins, her punctured arm, so much blood taken for innumerable tests, so much pain from the needle . . .

In the 1980s, she had been allergic to everything: pollen, dust in books, and probably me. Twice-weekly injections kept her allergies under control. Her body was a living wound. My Frida Kahlo. It seemed as though she could only survive in a world without plants. It's true that in her late childhood, her pre-allergic period, she didn't get along with plants either: she refused to drink tea . . . Every morning her parrot, Charlie, would repeat the only sentence he knew how to pronounce: "Drink your tea, Sanja! Drink your tea, Sanja!"

When we moved to D.C., her allergy returned for a while—because of the swirling winds that spin dust and pollen around in the basin between the Atlantic and the Appalachian chain—and she had allergy tests. The doctor in

Vienna scratched four long rows on her back with needle pricks (testing for all possible kinds of allergy) and for a while she bore those scars on her left shoulder blade like Angelina Jolie's tattoos.

But where is the pain from her past now? And where is the pain I concealed?

The woman who takes her blood at five in the morning announces herself from the doorway loudly enough to wake us: "Blood work!" She's called Dora Castro.

Today Sanja's right arm is numb, so she no longer feels the needle prick. And I'm glad it doesn't hurt her, but I'd like it to hurt her. All my senses have gone haywire.

This evening we are doing qigong in the ward with Asim, a doctor who believes in traditional Chinese medicine. A nurse came in and found us in the middle of our exercises, which resembled a sacred tribal ritual, and she left the room, walking slowly backward so as not to disturb anything. And later, when she came back to take Sanja's pulse, she made my day by asking: "Are you a Native American?"

Shared remembering, a precious part of our relationship, has pretty much vanished. How can I now restore to her memory the important days that should not be forgotten? Not the big, important events, but hundreds of tiny ones that we have reminded each other of over the years. Once we were driving in New Mexico, and if you looked through the window on the left-hand side of the car you saw a lovely sunny day; but if you looked through the right-hand one there was rain pouring down the pane. A quite unique moment of pure beauty! What if she's forgotten it forever? But how good that she doesn't remember all those sad and difficult days. There would be justice in their remaining forever in oblivion.

"Are you related?" asks a nurse.

"She's my wife."

But when I say, "She's my wife," that is a simplification, she's more than that. For instance, in 1993, during the siege of Sarajevo, a murderer pointed the barrel of a Kalashnikov at my chest. And she stepped between the gun and me.

"What happened to me?"

"Early in the morning on the second of April, it was raining. I decided to make coffee. You got up from the sofa and went to the bathroom. I spooned finely ground coffee into the filter, then I poured water into the machine, and then I heard a cry from the bathroom, your voice. But ten seconds earlier you had been laughing! I went to the bathroom and found you doubled up, you said your arm was numb and you couldn't feel your hand or your fingers. Shall we call an ambulance? No! You came back to the sofa, but when you tried to lie down the pain got worse, so you sat up again. I called an ambulance. They came quickly, but when I opened the door they complained about the long corridor they had to walk along. Our building has an incomprehensibly long corridor. 'By the time you've walked down that corridor, the patient might have died,' said a young man in a blue uniform. They took you to the hospital, a scan showed that you'd suffered a stroke. And here we are now on the oncology ward, they thought you had cancer, but that's wrong . . ."

The fingers of my right hand are swollen. I can bear pain, I've learned. The cold in Sarajevo during the siege years brought on my arthritis, which has gotten quite a bit worse over the last two years. It attacks me in the shoulder and the hip with horrible pain lasting from eight to ten hours. Or, as now, the inflammation makes my fingers stiff. In October last year I was at a literary gathering in Richmond. Wonderful weather, an Indian summer, and then on the first night I was woken by arthritis, my left shoulder was inflamed, unbearable pain; I stood by the window, rigid, in one position, looking out at the illuminated street. Young people were returning from nightclubs, laughing and tipsy, they passed my window the whole night, loud and drunk, and how I envied them their youth and health. In the morning, when Sanja was already awake and getting ready for work, I phoned her to say I was in pain and could hardly wait for the pharmacy to open, I'd go and buy some of those "hot patches" that you stick on the sore place to relieve the pain, and she told me to open my bag, because she'd already packed them in case I needed them. That's how I lived all these years. I'd call her so she could tell me what I had in my bag.

Every day I reach for Sanja's documents, because I'm often asked to fill in some new papers for which they need her personal details. That's how I've acquired the right to peer into her backpack and wallet. She always carries a backpack, she never got into the habit of carrying a traditional woman's handbag, but always, as long as I've known her, she has replaced that with a canvas bag or rucksack. All these American years she has worn her rucksack on her back to work and on journeys, but also on short outings to a restaurant or café. It's a serious burden, there are hundreds of things in it and, as she puts it, a dozen little things that make her feel confident. For instance, she has to have reserve earrings, because earrings get lost and she feels unprotected if she finds herself in a public space without earrings. One of her acquaintances once confided in me that she had been known to pull a button off a blouse just so that she could ask Sanja to sew it on again. Of course she has a needle and threads of various colors in her rucksack. The young American who pulls her buttons off had in fact never before witnessed the process of sewing on buttons: she was used to throwing away any garment with a missing button and buying another. But that was not the only reason for her need to watch the drawing of thread through a needle. Whenever Sanja sews a button onto a shirt of mine I, too, watch entranced, so I understand her American acquaintance. In my case, sewing a button on is an important image from my childhood that restores harmony to the world. Something in that act really awakens primordial memories.

There's a photograph of me in her wallet. I didn't know she carried my image around with her. It's not a portrait, a photo for a passport or other ID, such as often ends up in a wallet, but a cheerful snap of me holding a dog in my arms, and it isn't clear who looks happier or stupider in the photo, me or the dog. People put photographs of their nearest and dearest into their wallets out of inertia, but do they ever look at them? There are moments when we turn to those photographs, in a state of loneliness, traveling, when we are separated from those closest to us. I try to imagine her (in the past) opening her wallet and glancing at this snap. And what could my picture have meant to her at that moment?

A message on her phone: "Dear Sanja, the post offices are not working today, do you happen to know, please, what other shops sell stamps?" She's a little encyclopedia of practical solutions.

I'm keeping watch at her bedside. Three days have passed now. I have never loved her more. But, actually, that's not right. I've forgotten. It was the same during the war, it was the same whenever the presence of a catastrophe encroached on our relationship. That's only apparently a paradox, a tragic event increases our inner strength and our capacity for love. I keep watch at her bedside. I am an old, sentimental soldier.

I have no biography. A friend emailed me from Zagreb and asked: "'How is S.?" He doesn't know her. Or, rather, he knows her only as S., the way I most frequently used to refer to her in my texts. He was inquiring not about the health of my wife, but about the health of my literary character. I had already described almost everything important that had happened to me in my prose and poems, turning almost my entire life into fiction. It was now a collection of illusions, fairly unreliable, so that it would be hard to construct a factual account of my life. For years I've been transforming your body into words. That's my infidelity.

The sound of scanning the bar code on her plastic wristband is accompanied by the question:
    "Name and date of birth?"
    She says nothing.
    "What year is this?" asks the doctor.
    She says nothing.
    "What month is it?"
    She says nothing.

I ask her: "Who wrote the line 'April is the cruellest month . . .'"

And she says: "T. S. Williams."

It's interesting that she has merged T. S. Eliot and William Carlos Williams into one person. There must be a specific reason for that, but I'll think about that later, now I hurry to put her right: "Not Williams, but Eee . . ."

And she says: "Eliot! T. S. Eliot!"

In other words, she can't remember the calendar year, or the month in which we are now, but she does remember a line from a poem, and the name of the poet.

When we were left alone in the room, she became a child seeking attention, saying: "I was in such pain this morning!"

"What was hurting?" I asked, anxiously.

"I can't remember now, but something must have hurt."

Every ten minutes they come to take her blood, check her pulse, measure her blood pressure, at midnight they move her eight stories down to take a new image of her heart, then finally take her back to her room (the bed is her vehicle through the labyrinth of hospital corridors). They collect facts about her, but I'm not convinced that all this information is scrutinized and taken into account, because every new person who appears in our hospital room starts all over again with the same questions, informing him- or herself about everything from the start. We repeat endlessly the same series of events that brought us to the hospital. And, since the thrombosis was found in an artery on her left side, the cardiologist has insisted on restricting all activity with her left arm. This means that she can't have her blood pressure taken on that side, or blood taken out of those veins. And a new person really does come every ten minutes to take blood, and a new nurse to measure her blood pressure, and each time they move toward her left arm, and each time I stop them and tell them about the embargo, which they ought to know about. In other words, if I didn't inform them about her diagnosis, they would forever be doing the wrong thing. A "database" is an American obsession. To collect new data, medical staff come into the room every five minutes, so for four nights now Sanja has not had a wink of sleep. It's the third day since she has not had any water to drink or anything to eat, I smuggle ice cubes in for her to suck.

I ask the doctor: "Why can't she drink water, or eat?"

"Because she has had a stroke and the speech therapist has to confirm that she can swallow water and food correctly."

"So why doesn't the speech therapist come to establish that?"

"He's scheduled for tomorrow."

In a hospital, a body is exposed to systematic abuse, every ten minutes new facts are collected in a database, which, as far as one can judge, no one consults and is largely useless.

And why is a doctor's signature on prescriptions for medication always illegible?

I clasp her small tennis shoes in my hand. I was looking for a label, the name of the company that produces them, but I didn't find one. It's not known who produced them, or where they were made. There's no information about their origin. They are made of white canvas, the cheapest. Nameless. That's so like her! Because she buys things in spite of their branding: so if an iPhone, say, is the most popular of all mobiles, she will deliberately choose a different one, the one that is least shouted about. It's not always a satisfactory choice. That's why she now has a rather crass and unnecessarily complicated telephone, and, since she's begun to forget things, she's finding it ever more problematic to use it with each day.

She woke up and asked: "What are you doing with my shoes?" Good question. I must look pretty crazy peering at her tennis shoes like this. They're just shoes to her. And that's how it is: all her shoes have the same name, and there's no distinction between dress shoes and tennis shoes, they're all shoes to her.

Come to think of it, at our first meeting I was attracted by this absence of snobbism of hers. At that first meeting a group of people were discussing art. And then a girl—whose name I've since forgotten—had just returned from Paris and was talking enthusiastically about the work of her favorite painter, Toulouse-Lautrec. And Sanja, with the same enthusiasm for the painter and for one of his works in particular, went to the shelf and came back with *The History of World Art* open at that painting of Toulouse-Lautrec's. But her collocutor shook her head and said: "Yes, yes, but . . . No, no, that's not it" (that was the snob in her speaking, she had seen the *actual* painting, while the one in the book was just a reproduction), and she had already lost interest in the conversation about art, but Sanja pressed her finger onto the picture and, to her collocutor's horror, said: "Well, fuck that!" and went on talking about the painter. My kind of girl. My clever girl. My anti-snob!

When she went for her CT scan, because she was restless and kept moving her head, I stayed with her, wearing a lead apron to protect me from the radiation, holding her hand. And today, when we went for an MRI scan, in-depth imaging about which I had known nothing until now, I proposed to the girl who works there that I should again stay with the patient, to hold her hand and keep her calm. The girl laughed and said that wasn't possible, and when I asked why not, she said it was forbidden because the room where the MRI scan took place was like a shooting gallery, and you could be killed in there, because, she said, for instance, "if there was so much as the tiniest earring in the patient's ear, the magnet would reject it with such force that it would lodge in the wall, like a bullet from a gun."

"What kind of magnet?" I asked naively.

"This is an MRI machine," she said. "Do you know what the M in MRI stands for?"

"No."

"It means *magnetic*. MRI is magnetic resonance imaging."

"Well, OK," I say to justify my ignorance, "but wouldn't it be a beautiful, unique death, to be killed by her earring?"

The girl laughed, she found my ignorance entertaining.

A sunny morning. In the hospital parking lot a gardener is pushing Williams Carlos Williams's red wheelbarrow in front of him.

I've spent the whole day recalling Kafka's drawings and thinking of his *Diaries*. While Sanja sleeps, I keep vigil, I do nothing. I wait, although I'm not entirely sure what I'm waiting for. I supervise the nurses to make sure they don't accidentally give her the wrong medicine or take blood from the "wrong" arm. Then I feel useful. I look through the window at the rainy sky. Life is slowly turning into Kafka's syntax, in which there is no future tense. Who was it who said Kafka was a continent, and when you read him you always come to places where you've never been before? I've never before

longed like this for the outside world in which the two of
us visit places where we've never been before. A longing for
a time when everything was normal. From my perspective,
that was ten days ago, but for her it was several years ago,
before the time she has forgotten.

I want to believe that her memory will soon come back,
because we don't have the strength to fight against forgetting.

Over the last twelve days, I've realized that people no longer
call one another by telephone, they don't talk in real time,
just send one another text messages. That's not so bad. The
telephone rarely rings, I talk to the rest of the world in silence,
so that I don't wake her when she's sleeping. From the age of
speech, we have moved into the age of text. But I now need a
collocutor who would be prepared to listen to me for hours, a
bottle of good Dalmatian wine, and maybe a cigarette.

She thinks she's still a smoker, so today she asked: "Can I
go outside and light up over a coffee?"

She lit her last cigarette four years ago. The last four years
don't exist in her memory.

"After the stroke, you became four years younger!" I say.

I did try to draw her after all, but it didn't work. The reason
is simple: she has no awareness of it, or if she does, in the
next five minutes she'll forget that I'm drawing her. In a psy-
chological and a moral sense that's an impossible demand,

constantly to renew her agreement to being drawn, and every five minutes starting from scratch.

To reawaken memory, repetition is key, we have to renew everyday facts in the memory all over again, to recall the same events all over again. What year is this? Which month and day? She's well aware that she doesn't remember, and asks questions that are crucial to her, she turns to me out of her forgetfulness with full emotional participation. This is one question that she repeats every day: "How's your mother?"

"She died in December, four months ago," I say.

She starts to cry. "I didn't know . . . I'm sorry."

And she repeats the question "How's your mother?" every day. And every day she experiences with the same intensity the news she has forgotten, always hearing it for the first time.

It's after midnight already and I've been watching Pat O'Neill's film *The Decay of Fiction*. It's an experimental video about the abandoned Ambassador Hotel in Los Angeles. Documentary shots of empty corridors, the deserted night bar, and abandoned rooms alternate with shots of important events that took place in those same locations in the past. The film is edited so that space turns into time. And, as I watch, my anxiety grows, but nonetheless I can't stop staring at the screen, whose bluish light has woken Sanja. Her face is sweaty, she asks: "Can you bathe me?"

I wash her secretly, but you can't call it a bath. She looks uncomfortable when the nurses help her, while for their part they oppose everything that I myself do. This is not a regulation bath; it's impossible to separate her from the bed to which she is connected by transparent cables and the heart monitor. I have supplies of damp handkerchiefs and use them to refresh her. From her face to her feet. And now that we are old, I recall the girl she was. I run the damp handkerchiefs over her face, neck, and shoulders, over her breasts, under her arms, carefully down her arms so as not to shift the needle in her vein, not to touch the wounds from the puncture holes in her hand, then over her stomach, between her legs, and down her thighs, calves, ankles, and feet. This could look like a mournful erotic game in which the only important rule is that my movements should not cause her pain. Her body is familiar territory for me, it has altered with time, and I remember it in various phases. I remember *all* her bodies.

In the course of the night, between Saturday and Sunday, we have become old people. But can I imagine any other woman who would have grown old like this beside me?

The world has gone on living without us. Nothing has changed because we have gotten stuck on the eighth floor of a hospital, our hands leaning on a glass wall through which, from a height, we look down on the garden of a family home. A man in the middle of a telephone conversation walks across the lawn in front of the entrance, goes over to an oak at the end of the garden, leans his left hand against its trunk, and continues his conversation. It is a vision of an ordinary life that suddenly seems to me remote and inaccessible. We are practicing walking along the hospital corridor and have arrived at this glass wall, looking down at a family home in front of which a man is leaning his left palm against the trunk of an oak tree. Arlington is spread out below us, behind it is Falls Church, and beyond that Vienna and Tysons Corner. She draws a circle with a finger on the glass in front of her and says: "We used to live there. I remember. That's where the Institute of Subtitling Hollywood Films was." I stand beside her, my right hand leaning on the glass of the window, with the imprint of an oak's bark on my left palm . . .

It's almost dawn; we are looking at the hospital windowpane. She's glad that she's awake to watch the transition from night to day. She says there's a great contrast between light and darkness, people ought to watch the sunrise ritually, so the body can accept the abrupt change naturally. Through the window of the hospital room, we watch to see whether the sun will again rise in the east. It's not yet dawn, so the light from the room makes the glass in front of us into a mirror in which we see ourselves.

"I've grown old."

"You haven't grown old."

"I have, I have."

"No, you haven't."

"I have!"

"You haven't!"

"I have if I say so!"

And here is the sun.

"What happened to me?"

"It all happened early one morning, on the second of April. Saturday. It was raining. We had already had our morning coffee and I'd decided to make another. I asked you whether you wanted another, and you laughed and said you did. You got up from the sofa and went to the bathroom. Whenever I describe our room, I say *sofa*, but it isn't a sofa, it's a daybed, I don't know how we'd say that in our language, something to lie on that is higher and wider than a sofa, a *day*bed (as distinct from an ordinary bed which is primarily a *night* bed), because it's for lying down on before it gets dark. Most of the important events in our life have taken place in our language, but the most important ones have happened in English. Those are the days from which I never emerged. There aren't many of them. Three or four. I would like them not to have happened, I would like not to remember them, but that isn't possible. So, to describe that day, 2 April 2016, I ought to use English. You got up from the daybed and went to the bathroom, while I poured coffee into the filter. And while you were in the bathroom, your left arm went numb.

You couldn't feel your fingers and there was unbearable pain in your shoulder. It happened in an instant. You were fine, cheerful and talkative, and then came that sudden pain. I called an ambulance, they came quickly and after a cursory examination decided to take you to the hospital for a more detailed examination. And in the hospital, the CT and MRI scans showed that you have a clot in your left subclavian artery, which, in all probability, caused a stroke. Plus, it turned out that you are very anemic. All that is why we're here now."

"Can I ask you something?"

"Go ahead."

"When I die, please have me cremated. And then you absolutely must take me home," she says.

Fear of death in a foreign world. There had also been fear of life in a foreign world, but such fear is not so threatening or devastating. We all live with our own fear of death, but the important addition (*in a foreign world*) conveys a substantial, metaphysical unease, although there's an obvious paradox in it all: Why do we feel uneasy about a space in which we will in fact no longer be, simply because we will no longer exist? We aren't capable of thinking outside our own life. Even in death it's important to be at home.

We watch the snow through the window. Big flakes are falling. She has never liked snow, she has a horror of the cold, and that feeling was magnified in the freezing war years, during the siege of Sarajevo.

She looks through the window and asks: "What's this?"

I say: "Snowflakes."

"I've never seen such big snowflakes," she says.

"Nor have I," I say.

"Up to now we've only known *snowflakes*," she says, "these are our first *snowplates*."

A nurse came into the room, bringing medication. She scanned the bar code on her wristband and asked the routine questions that accompany that action: "Your name . . . ?"

"Sanja Mehmedinović."

"Date of birth . . . ?"

"September seventeenth . . ."

And then, looking out the high window at the snow falling outside, I asked: "And what month is this?"

She gazed at the snow through the window until she remembered: "April . . ." She began to cry. And she said: "'April is the cruellest month, breeding / Lilacs out of the dead land . . .' T. S. Eliot! I've remembered!"

The nurse looked at me, seeking an explanation, but I didn't know what to say.

Her speech is unchanged, her supply of words is the same. If language is a mirror of the world, then nothing that she has remembered (and now forgotten) is lost. If her language has been preserved in its entirety, then the whole world that has settled in her language has remained complete. That means she has forgotten *nothing* and now we have just to grab that *everything* back from oblivion.

My friend Ivica Puljić comes by this morning, he says he had a strange dream. "In my dream I'm eight years old, and it's as if I'm looking at myself from outside: I've got bangs cut at an angle, I'm in Sarajevo and I'm sitting on a low stone wall. Then my father comes up to me, he's young and handsome, and he says: 'Come on, I'm taking you away from here.' 'Where to?' I ask. 'To the Vatican.' After that we're in the square at the Vatican and we come to a wall, which is in fact that same wall from Sarajevo. 'Sit here,' my father says, 'and wait for me.' And I sat and waited, but he didn't come back."

Ivica . . . Since I've been in America, he's been my older brother who walks behind me, correcting my mistakes.

Harun called from the plane, saying that he wasn't going to land at DCA (as he had first told me), he was going to land at Dulles. He hadn't looked carefully at the ticket he'd bought in a hurry. I emerged from the hospital garage into a sunny day.

Dulles is pronounced like *Dallas* and once, in the distant 1980s, a friend from Zagreb, on his first visit to Washington and America, became agitated when, some twenty minutes before landing, the captain informed his passengers over the loudspeaker that they would soon be landing in *Dallas*. And my friend was convinced that he would be landing in Texas, that he was on the wrong plane, and that made him pretty agitated. I'm thinking of his traveler's nerves as I drive to the airport, because that's how I'm feeling now: as though everything that's happening to me is the consequence of a misunderstanding of which I have just become aware, and that "just" has been going on for days now, and profound anxiety has become my normal state.

On the way to the airport, I drove through Peach Tree, past the building where we lived in 1996 and 1997. I looked at the parking lot in front of the building, and an image surfaced out of oblivion. I had bought our first car, we're in the parking lot, it's snowing, Harun is pestering me to let him drive, "only over there to the library building and back." "Go on," I say. He's thirteen, he's driving a car for the first time, and, with an expression of pure joy on his child's face, he watches the regular motion of the windshield wipers in front of him. And now, twenty years later, as I drive to the airport, I see *that* smile of his. Instinctively, I want to turn time back. I imagined a present for you, my son, in which you constantly experience things for the first time.

In the airport Starbucks, I bought a coffee, went to the luggage conveyor belt, and sat down on its metal edge. There are no tense travelers around me, just the occasional airport official passes with a walkie-talkie in which crackling human voices vanish. And then I remember that less than a year ago, before her flight to Sarajevo, Sanja and I sat in this same place, drinking coffee from paper cups. That means that I came instinctively to precisely this place, so great is my need to be close to her. At this moment, all the events of my life exist in unison in space. So all my presents exist constantly. I wait for Harun. At last he appears in a group of other people, with a red bandana on his head. He stops for a moment, to call someone. And then the telephone in my pocket rings, beside my heart.

Harun is sitting opposite her, at the end of the bed. She tells him he's thin and asks: "What do you eat, what do you live off, sweetheart?" He tells her he has a lot of work and eats what he can along the way. There's something obvious in the relationship between mother and son, something irrevocable, but every time I try to describe it, I become confused and tongue-tied. I get up from the chair and in the mirror on the wall see myself, I see the bed on which she is lying, and our son resting his hand on the edge of the bed. I see the three of us captured in the mirror so clearly, as though we are in the wasteland of the cosmos, warming each other with our hands. Three, we're plural, but at the same time, in the mirror we're the reflection of pure isolation. She looks at her son as though she hasn't seen him for years (literally, because her last memory of him is several years old) and says she loves him "with a whole universe of mouse footsteps."

In April of last year, Harun and I roamed through the American wilderness for a project he was working on at the time, taking photographs of the starry sky. I remember one black night, we had stopped somewhere just before midnight. In the darkness I had the impression that I was at the very end of the world, and I recall our vigil till morning as an experience filled with isolation and sublime solitude. It was only in the morning that the view burst into life before my eyes, and what the cameras had been recording during the night were three red rocks in the valley and the sky above them. Monument Valley. A month later, in May, those shots were shown on a jumbotron behind Mick Jagger and Keith Richards during the Rolling Stones' Zip Code tour as a visual illustration of the song "Moonlight Mile." What a giant step from solitude to non-solitude! Something that came into being in maximum isolation from the world had become part of a public, global event.

My body remembers various kinds of solitude, but none has laid me waste like this as I sit awake through the night by her bedside, watching her tormented by pain and insomnia.

A new novel by Ian McEwan is due out in September. In the book, the writer describes his unborn child hearing in his mother's womb a conversation in which someone was plotting a murder. Memory begins before our birth. But how could an unborn child remember words whose meaning he doesn't know when he hears them? Unless he has a photographic memory, so he recalled the words by their sound and only later was their meaning revealed.

Sanja used to have a photographic memory, the gift (or curse) of visually recalling whole pages of a book. But that disappeared with Harun's birth. In the later months of her pregnancy the doctor explained that "the fetus was draining her," and she said: "This child is stronger than me!"

She was always the one who took care of me, rather than the other way around. It's hard to change roles. She lies in her hospital bed, looks at me, and asks: "Is there anything I can do for you?"

And when the doctor asks her something that she can't recall, she begins to behave as though she were at a school exam, she looks at me, raising her eyebrows for me to whisper the answer.

"What's your name?"
"Sanja."
"Date of birth?"
"September seventeenth."
"What day is it today?"

"I'm not sure . . ."

"What's the name of our president?"

She tries in vain to remember his name, then describes: "One of those two . . . from the same family . . ." (She's thinking of Bush.)

"Think," I say, "the current president is the first African American in the White House . . ."

"Wow! That's a real improvement!" And then she does remember: "Obama!"

I sit by her bed, gradually becoming obsessed with forgetfulness.

We discover something about time as we watch what it does to our body. Or watch a child growing beside us. But our body is not proof that time exists. And the problem is not that we forget, but that we remember. Quantitative physics does not recognize continuity. But our experience is precisely an experience of continuity. That's an insoluble problem. We remember what happened yesterday.

Renata came to visit this morning. She sat beside her and did useful things the whole time; for instance, she began massaging her face. She evidently knows how to behave in the company of a patient, while I looked on, endeavoring to remember all her actions, so as to be able to repeat them myself later. But that massaging of her face looked like a ritual, and she described everything she was doing in a whisper, explaining why it was important to apply pressure above the brow bone, and then she pressed the area under her eye sockets. I'm very sensitive where eyes are concerned. On rainy days when I'm in the street and people come toward me with umbrellas, the pressure in my eyes increases. I'm wary of those metal spokes, one of which could damage my eye. It's an irrational fear, one of those formed in childhood. When Renata presses her left thumb into the soft flesh below Sanja's right eye, I instinctively close my eyes.

The question is: Where does the time go? Forgetfulness is not only the disappearance of events from the past but also the complete erasure of time. When I ask her what year it is, she doesn't know, and when I say it is 2016, she's surprised: Where did so many years go? And she asks: "Where did the time go?"

"It went."

"It went to its own home."

In a hospital the most important fact about us is the year of our birth. But in our lives that year is of no particular importance. I had to grow old to understand that. Everyone dies young.

The therapist is in the room now, and they've been doing memory exercises for half an hour already. She's placing photographs on the mobile bed table in front of her. Four photographs show a man shaving in a bathroom. Her task is to arrange the images in the right order. The first one shows the face with a week-old beard, the next applying shaving cream, then the act of shaving, and the last in that succession is a photograph of a man wiping his shaved face with a small towel. A consequence of the stroke is the slow connection of actions in their continuity. Recovering from the stroke means speeding those connections up. But the problem with memory is precisely the loss of continuity. She hasn't forgotten, because, with a little prompting, I can bring her back to an event from the past, if she can't remember the name of Kendra's six-month-old baby, I say the Bosnian word for "queen," and then she says: "Quinn!" And then she corrects me: "*Quinn* is pronounced like *queen*, but Quinn is not a queen!" If she can't remember the name of the district of Sarajevo where we lived during the war, I begin: "Seddd . . ." And she says: "Sedrenik!" She hasn't forgotten, it just takes effort to remember. I watch her trying to arrange the photographs in front of her in the correct order. And she isn't certain whether to place the last photo on the table in front of her in the first place, the one of the man wiping his washed face with a green towel.

My morning shave is a riddle connected with remembering for me as well. This is the rule: After washing, I apply soap to my wet skin, and at the same moment as I begin to scrape it off with my razor, into my consciousness comes Z., a little girl from primary school. She had an afro hairstyle and an unnaturally short space between her top lip and her nose. It's not an early romance that connects me to her. But whenever I shave, her face appears so vividly in my consciousness, just as though she were standing behind me and her reflection could be seen in the mirror. Why does this happen? I don't know. There's no answer to the reasons for our memories. There's no answer even when it's a question of our earliest memories.

The doctor has a brightly colored tie with cheerful children's drawings on it so that he conveys a positive, relaxed impression to the patients. That must be the case, as Sanja immediately compliments him on the colorfulness of his tie. She ends her praise by announcing that she has never seen anything like it. The doctor then asks: "Are there no ties in your country?" Those kinds of questions always strike a nerve with her, offensive questions foreigners here have to answer in the first years of their exile. ("Do people drive cars in your country?") "Well now, doctor, the tie as a fashion item was invented in my country, the word *cravat* comes from the Croats, who wore them as part of their military uniform in the sixteenth century!" The doctor is surprised at her explanation, he listens patiently to her lecture, then he quietly takes the edge of his tie between his thumb and forefinger and pulls it out of his white coat so that it can be seen in all its colorfulness, on his chest.

✦

Her sight has deteriorated. At the same time, her sight has improved. I don't know how else to say this. For instance: She no longer needs reading glasses, but when she looks at me she sees dark hollows on my face. To start with, immediately after the stroke, she couldn't see anything on the right side of her field of vision, she kept touching the edge of her eye, as though something there was preventing her from seeing and she was trying to remove it with her hand. One evening her eye was irritating her so much that I bathed it in sterilized water. So, the dark patches that appear on the edge of her field of vision are particularly irritating. The experts say that the brain is a flexible and transformative machine. Sometimes she'd say: "That's strange, on my right I'm now seeing geometric shapes and the faces of people who aren't in the room." So what's actually going on? Her mind is drawing images from her memory and building them into the dark patches of her vision so as to accustom her to seeing a whole, in fact convincingly deceiving her that there are no patches, no empty spaces; her gaze is filled up with images from the past, or objects from her imagination. For a week now she has not complained of darkness on her right side and maintains that she can see.

I'm becoming irritable, and the medical staff avoid me. Even my own hair is a burden. I had somehow to injure myself, so as not to injure anyone else. Last night, when Sanja had fallen asleep, I went to the bathroom and cut my hair with my razor. My first thought was to shave it all off, but my courage failed me when I looked in the mirror.

This morning Ivica came with a bouquet of flowers. She's sleeping, so we whisper. There's no vase, just a tall glass. But for the flowers to fit into the glass, we have to cut off the firm green stems. Ivica shortens them with a knife. And suddenly, I have a sense image of human hair being cut with an ax.

The hospital bed squeaks every time one of us leans a hand on the protective rail. If one of us gets up and tries to extract ourself from it, the bed alarms the nurses on duty and they hurry into the room. I understand the purpose, but this is way over the top, every movement sets off a shrill alarm that in the late-night hours freezes the blood in our veins, maddens us both, makes me jumpy, and her, too, I presume. And then this evening it happened that the bed squeaked and no nurse came. They object if I do their job, but now I have every reason to be dissatisfied with their work. And why is that noise so irritating? The bed has its consciousness, but its cleverness creates more damage than benefit. Its basic concept is, of course, very useful—an alarm that can protect the patient from potential self-harm. But in reality it is, on the whole, a machine for nocturnal torture.

✦

We have moved too often, the last time two years ago, in February 2014. It's not advisable to move in the winter, because rain or snow might fall on your household furniture, on the bed or books. We moved only a few miles to the north, over here, near the river, and on the way the young men who were transporting our things—in a moving truck rented for the occasion—lost our bed. In every move, something is lost along the way, a box of books, a shirt. But how can you lose a bed? It's not an umbrella. A bed is too big to disappear like that. "Where's the bed?" I asked the young men taking our things out of the truck, but they just shrugged their shoulders, perplexed.

The doctor (the one with the cheerful tie) presented me painstakingly with the problem that awaited us when we left the hospital: she would have to come every day for injections of warfarin (an anticoagulant), but it could all be made simpler if I agreed to give her the injections at home. "Impossible, I'm terrified of injections," I say. I could have succumbed to any addiction, but not heroin. "A syringe? No, no, no way."

"Would you not try?"

"Out of the question."

That conversation disturbed me, because driving every day to the hospital would be exhausting for both of us. Besides, I can't ask at work for several hours off to do that every day. I mean, I can ask, but who would approve it? That same evening, Sanja complained of pain, where they give her the injections, three fingers to the left or three fingers to the right of her navel. Here they do it mechanically and roughly. She was sleeping when the nurse appeared at midnight, and I asked: "Can I give her the injection?" The nurse had been present at my conversation with the doctor, so she agreed readily. It calmed me that Sanja was asleep, so that at least I wouldn't see the pain on her face when I did it. The nurse explained the whole process slowly and patiently. It wasn't light enough in the room, I didn't dare give an injection in the half darkness, so I turned on all the lights in the room, which woke Sanja. Alarmed, she looked at me gripping the syringe with rigid fingers. I said: "I'm going to give you your injection, so that it hurts less." I said that more to encourage myself, but it soothed her. The needle was really barely visible, with a straight prick, and without moving the syringe it couldn't hurt (much). It all happened quickly, because I wanted to get it over as soon as possible, the nurse praised me, the way one compliments a child who has successfully carried out a task. And Sanja said: "It didn't hurt at all!"

"Listen," I say. "I went to all your scans, CT, MRI, with you. I was beside you, wearing a lead apron in the midst of the radiation, I held your hand as long as it lasted! Now, is that love or isn't it, you tell me?"

"Cut it out," she says. "Stop dicking around!" (That's a

phrase she uses as a translation of an expressive Bosnian colloquialism with that meaning.)

Thinner, in a new outfit, a blue-gray silk blouse and a gray knee-length skirt, with sunglasses and a new hairdo, she went out into the sun and looked around, bewildered, as though she were seeing the world for the first time.

"Look at you," I say, "like a Hollywood diva on her way home from rehab!"

She laughs and says: "Melanie Griffith!"

We're on our way home from the hospital; as we come onto George Mason Drive, she gazes at the houses along the road: "I've never been here before! It's all unfamiliar." Then we turn into Columbia Pike, the street in which we lived a little more than two years ago and along which we drove to and from work. I watch her reactions, waiting for her to recognize something, anything . . . We pass a place called Rappahannock Coffee, and she says: "I came here once with Kendra!" She began to remember. I want to believe that— once she gets back to her own world, to the intimacy of her apartment, and when she comes again into contact with her neighborhood, with places where she has often been—she will remember everything. I really believe this, and I'm impatient for it to happen, for her focus to return and for her finally to relax back into her own world. And the fact that she recognized a café in which she may have been only once, that she remembered she was with her friend, that she had drunk coffee (which was good!), that she ate a croissant, just strengthens my conviction that her memory will be quickly restored. We drive toward the Pentagon, with the panorama of Washington behind it, it's the middle of April, but the sky is as blue as summer and I'm happy to be going home on such a lovely day. For me this is an omen, and, as we drive, I keep saying: "Everything's going to be all right." I ask her: "What can you see now?"

"The Pentagon," she says.

And the closer we get to the building where we live, her memory seems to me to be increasingly vivid.

But when I stop in the car park in front of the building, she asks: "How long have we lived here?"

"Two years."

"I don't remember it at all! This is the first time I've seen this building!"

We have come back. I open the front door, and our apartment smells of coffee.

It's almost midnight. Harun peers into the fridge looking for something sweet. He's after a particular taste from his mother's repertoire, but what is it? He can't remember. He tries to recall what that taste reminds him of. Then he does after all remember the Mexican dessert *tres leches*. Dough that draws sweetness into itself like a sponge; something like the *patišpanja* of his childhood. *Patišpanja* is a dessert that came to Bosnia from Spain—as its name suggests—brought by the Sephardim. The taste of *tres leches* is like *patišpanja*. Midnight and *patišpanja*. All these years she has done the cooking, now it's my turn. Am I capable? It was time to give her the last medication of the day, Lipitor. I woke her, she propped herself up and, half-asleep, took her medicine, then turned onto her other side. I covered her up, saying, like a prayer: "Darling Sanja, make us *patišpanja* . . ."

Haircut, hair dyeing. She insists on that, because she doesn't like the gray hairs that have begun to show at the edges, while I have long wanted her to let her natural hair grow. Renata came with scissors, and she is skilled with them, she cut Sanja's hair so that the right side is a little longer and falls naturally over her ear, while the shorter, left side is tucked behind her ear, it is even shorter at the nape, but the asymmetry turns out well, making her still lovelier. She had to have her hair cut shorter to make the days of her recuperation easier, and we opted for a style that in normal circumstances she would never have agreed to. I'm not certain that she'll like her new haircut, but I like it. When she bathed, I used to run my fingers through her hair. I've been repeating that action for thirty-five years now: running my fingers through her hair. She resists a little, because she has a cat's nature, while I must have a dog's because I like being touched. For thirty-five years she has fallen asleep gripping a lock of my hair in her hand. That's why I've let my hair grow long all this time, so that she can hold it while she sleeps.

It calms her to hold my hair . . . We kept moving house, the walls of our rooms kept changing, but there was always the same black-and-white photograph over the desk, taken by Mladen Pikulić way back in 1980. The photo is of her with V., her friend from her youth. They're standing side by side, shoulders touching, looking at the camera. She's wearing a white summer dress. A snowflake. In a white dress that reaches almost to her ankles, Sanja is standing on the tips of her left toes, while her right foot is invisible, leaning against the wall behind her. Her right arm is raised above her head, and she's holding a lock of hair in her clenched fist. But the hair is alive, and at the moment when the photograph was taken, half the lock had escaped from her hand. That is the only movement in the picture, probably visible and crucial only to me. Her need to hold on to hair is a consequence of her insecurity.

The first time I saw this photograph was in a small Sarajevo gallery, in a group exhibition, at the opening of which the then-unknown punk band Zabranjeno Pušenje provided the entertainment.

✦

Today on the internet I came across some scenes from a film by a young Colombian director called Ciro Guerra. In one scene a Western scientist shows a photograph to the shaman of an almost completely extinct tribe; the picturesque inhabitant of the Amazon is evidently seeing a photograph for the first time in his life, and then he looks at himself in the picture with interest, sees his necklace, then he looks at the same object on his chest and compares them. When the scientist tries to take the photograph out of his hands, the shaman is surprised and says: "What are you doing?"

"I'll keep this, it's mine."

"But this is me," says the confused shaman.

And then the scientist corrects him: "This isn't you. It's a picture of you."

Two opposed concepts of possession.

I sent the link to her email address, for her to see when she gets better. The two of us weren't made for this world, because there's nothing in it we want to possess. But now I realize that we're being punished: if I'd acquired property, we would have enough money for me to take her to a warmer place to sit on a bench or sunny balcony and watch the gleaming water.

A photograph gives shape to memory. When I look at my past, the way it exists in photos, it seems to me that I'm not just one, but several, perhaps even a dozen different people.

My friend Milomir Kovačević once sent me a photograph in an email and asked: "Do you remember when this was?" In the picture I'm very young, I'm sitting at a table, perhaps at a literary evening, or some such event. I had never seen that photograph before, and I don't remember the year when it was taken. Maybe 1984, or 1986, or 1988? In those years I used to wear a black sweater. Clothes lasted a long time, and I remember that sweater more clearly than myself in those days. I remember that Sanja bought the same sweater in white as well, as she couldn't decide on the color. I remember their smell. And so, over time, the sweater had become less of a stranger for me than the young man in the picture.

Tonight we went with Harun to Gravelly Point, a park beside the airport, because he wanted to take photographs of planes landing at night. It was still light when we got there, he walked in front of us, looking for a suitable place for his camera, while over his head flew a flock of butterflies, as though accompanying him. A dozen big monarchs! There should have been a photograph of them!

The monarch butterfly migrates from Mexico to Canada and then returns, but that migration takes four generations. The first generation migrates from Mexico to Texas, the third is born in Canada. The grandfather and grandchild butterflies live out their brief lives in different countries. Like those of us who are born in the Balkans.

✦

Two weeks ago Harun arrived at one airport (Dulles), and he is leaving from another (DCA). I'm uneasy about his departure. In our lives this is an event that is constantly repeated: driving each other to an airport. There have already been too many partings. I stop the car, we both get out for him to take his bag from the trunk and for us to say goodbye. A quick embrace ("Take care of yourself!" "You too!"), and he has already vanished through the automatic door that closes behind him so that I see my reflection in it.

And then, frozen there, gazing at the glass airport door, I was greeted by an acquaintance; he was glad to see me. I was still sad, affected by our parting, but this man was genuinely glad that we had met. I recognized him, but I couldn't remember his name. We used to meet outside the Voice of America building when we both worked there. Many years had passed since then. He was otherwise a passionate reader of poetry, and at those smoking breaks we talked on the whole about poetry. Once he brought me *Recollections of Gran Apacheria* by Edward Dorn, to show me the sketches in the book and the photograph on the last page, so as to convince me that Dorn and I were so alike we could have been twins. What was his name? I endeavored not to let him see my embarrassment. He reproached me for not getting in touch since I left the Voice of America. In the end, he grew sad and told me he had cancer. I didn't know what to say. I never know what to say when I hear tragic news. Where was he going? San Diego. I have forgotten his name, but I remember that he used to underline important passages in his books with a graphite pencil.

She forgot to give Harun a ducat; she remembered after he left. "So, you remember that gold coin?"

"Of course I do!"

I'm glad every time she remembers something recent. It means that her forgetting is not amnesia, she has lost focus, but when she is reminded of an event, an image is then awakened in her and so plucked from oblivion. She bought that ducat this year, in January I think, or February, but she had forgotten where she put it, she searched all the places where the little box with the gold coin in it might have been but didn't find it.

And she said: "Come to think of it, the ducat is something that otherwise doesn't exist. A ducat as a nonexistent unit of measurement. In our language a clever person would be praised with the saying 'All his ducats have value.' The closest we got to a ducat was when a factory started producing chocolate in the shape of a coin. Did you go digging in your garden, looking for nonexistent treasure? We all dug and searched for gold coins in our childhood. The ducat was a measure of value from the past, the nineteenth century presumably. And we all referred to gold ducats, without ever having actually seen one. That's why I bought that gold coin with the face of Mark Twain on it as a gift for Harun, so that a ducat would be a nonexistent measure of value for him, a metaphor, as it had been for us. I put it somewhere in the house, but where? I don't know, I've been searching all morning, but I can't find it. He often quotes Mark Twain on his Facebook page, the two of them were born on the same day . . ."

Varnishing her nails. I paint her nails. I'm slow and I don't move calmly from the root of the nail to the tip, I'm not exactly a skillful painter. But she doesn't object. She has small, child's hands; when her nails are painted black, they look like watermelon seeds. Today's color is: yellow.

Existing in the consciousness of a child. "Once Zara, a little girl of five, saw a woman with yellow nail polish and a yellow scarf. Zara is now a grown woman and she often remembers that unusual woman with yellow nails waiting for a bus at the Huntington Terrace stop. The little girl grew up with that image . . ."

"And who's the woman with yellow nails?"

"You."

Drawing a clock. This morning I managed to persuade her to draw a clock face: to write in the numbers and draw the hands so that she can see what time it is now. Yesterday she put the 12 and 6 in the right places, only she swapped the numbers from the left with the ones from the right. But this morning they are all in the right place, except that she has written 9 where she should have put 3 and 3 where 9 should have been. She is still mixing up the left and right side.

Ina, my boss from the German television station, sent flowers, a lovely bunch of tulips.

(This year in Arlington, deer have been going into gardens and eating the flowers. Not any flowers, they are selective, and they are particularly fond of tulips. It hasn't ever happened before that deer came into people's gardens for their flowers. Or at least the owners of Arlington gardens don't remember them doing so.)

Ina once wrote out a text for me on a sheet of paper so that her writing could only be read in a mirror. As a child in her first year at school she wrote with her left hand; later she was taught to write with her right, but she could never be dissuaded from mirror writing. The left and right sides of her brain are in perfect harmony.

I look at the clock that Sanja has drawn on a sheet of white paper and think: If these notes about her should ever be published in a book, then the text should be printed so that the words can be read in a mirror placed next to the open pages.

How long will our process of recovery last? A telephone call from Vermont. Among all the other health advice, D. says that Sanja ought to eat walnuts—"They are good for the brain," D. says. "It's no coincidence that the kernel of a walnut looks so like a brain!"

I brush her hair and dress her. To start with, I chose my own T-shirts and shirts, because they're roomier than her tops, which made it easier for me, and I confess that I like seeing her in my clothes. But I soon discovered she has quite a rich collection of light summer dresses. I choose a new one for going out in every day. I brush her hair the way I think her hairdo should be arranged, and she doesn't object, she accepts my choice of dress for the day, she is slowly being transformed into a little girl and I into her older brother. An inversion of our ages. When we met, we were serious and old beyond our years, but then we began to grow backward and now we are two weary, frightened children.

After an absence of three weeks, I went back to work: she stayed alone in the apartment and that worried me. She began writing a diary, in which she noted small domestic events, so as not to forget them in the course of the day. And I want to believe that this is one of the ways that her new memory can begin to be formed. She's alone at home, and I'm anxious and keep going out to get a coffee. Over the entrance to our building, the one where I work, they've installed a closed-circuit camera. Inside, in the corridor, they had put up a small flat monitor so that the screen shows the pavement outside the entrance from a bird's-eye perspective. As I come back from the café, I open the door and take a few steps toward the screen and always see myself in front of the building, opening the door and coming in. That's because, in relation to reality, the image is delayed by a full eight seconds. We don't know why. But always when I come back in, I hurry to the screen so as to observe my entrance into the building more carefully. And I see it with a child's interest, because it's pleasing to see oneself in a past that's only eight seconds old but hasn't yet become a memory.

At midnight, my left arm became numb, it must be a new heart attack. So now what? I get out of bed carefully so as not to wake Sanja. It's really not good. It's not the right time for an infarct. The arm's quite numb. I search in my bag for the nitroglycerine tablet I carry with me in case my heart seizes up like this, it should help for a while. I put the little bottle with the tablet in front of me on the desk. Then I open up the unfinished texts on my desktop computer, intending to email them to Harun, to protect them from the chaos of multiple versions, so that in the future no one would mistakenly print texts I wasn't yet happy with. Those small tasks soothed me, although my arm was increasingly stiff. I opened the piece I'd been working on for months now, corrected one or two typos, altered the occasional sentence, and then I added a whole new fragment. When I'd finished it, I read through what I had written and was satisfied, and that stimulated my desire to write. I stayed awake until morning, making notes. And at daybreak I filled the kettle with water for our first coffee. Outside it was drizzling.

They say that troubles never come singly, other, smaller or greater problems graft themselves onto them. And that is indeed the case. Of all the additional troubles that occurred over recent days, the one that most disturbs me is the alarm on our car, because it has suddenly begun to go on and off of its own accord, bothering people around us. It happens unexpectedly, sometimes after midnight, or early in the morning. There's no logic to the activation of the alarm. Our car is a Ford Taurus, made in 2002, and on the internet I found that the unusual behavior of the alarm was a factory fault. That happens with American cars, in a culture founded on a quick profit, cars are built with cheap components, so as to make savings in their production and produce the maximum profit. In any case, the alarm went off uncontrollably and this caused me a significant problem. I accustomed my ear to its sound, I wake easily and dash down to turn it off, and then come slowly back up the stairs. Sometimes it happens that on my way back I hear it again, so I go back down. Horrible! I am becoming afraid of our Taurus. Today I fell asleep from tiredness, and now her voice summons me from sleep: "Wake up, Sem, the car's whistling again!"

Our alarm that turns itself on and off rhythmically.

Sanja's stroke occurred in the English language. In these notes I translate the whole event into an isolated, fairly remote language (spoken by a relatively small number of people, so that I can imagine its future disappearance). Some details are not translatable. Our isolation is seen most clearly in the empty space between the two languages. But that empty space is the same as forgetting.

At work, on my lunch break, I go up onto the roof with my salad, I sit in the shade of a large satellite disk, and at the level of my gaze there's a placard proclaiming BLUES ALLEY. That's a jazz bar where I used to go in 1996 and 1997, twenty years ago. I was working at the Voice of America then. And I always used to go there after midnight, when my night shift finished. The music would have stopped, the guests were dispersing, the musicians packing up their instruments. I used to come here because of a delusion: under the blue light of the bar, at the end of the day, I could be one of them, musicians, free night birds, and not a bewildered immigrant. I haven't been there for nearly twenty years. But now almost every day, if it isn't too cold or if it isn't raining, I sit on the roof just after midday, opposite the bar. It's in a very narrow alley and if I were to stretch I could reach the whiteboard inscribed BLUES ALLEY. In fact, all my past is always here, just across the road and within reach. If I were to take off properly, I would be able to jump into it from this roof.

After two months of not setting foot in a bookshop, we went to Barnes and Noble. Two months without the aroma of books. She walks behind me explaining: "There's nothing in this shop. They only have books that sell well here." She's right, but I need to breathe in the smell of paper, for it to restore my balance, and I wanted to buy Don DeLillo's new novel (*Zero K*, which went on sale yesterday). I easily found the book on the shelf, but the design and layout of the text put me off. I think I'd find it tiring to read. That happens to me with certain books, they are made ineptly so that they become an unattractive object. I'd like to read the new novel, but my eyes resist it. We went out as warm rain began to fall. It moistened the body agreeably. It was too hot in the car, the windows misted up from inside. As we were leaving the parking lot a motorbike materialized right in front of me, with a woman hugging the driver around the waist. Two old people, in fact. When the rider appeared in front of me he was so close that I first saw his frightened face and heard him scream. It was only thanks to that scream that I instinctively trod on the brake, they passed in front of us, and I paused for a few seconds before we went on. I watched that old couple in front of us, he seemed confused and kept changing lanes uncontrolledly, I skirted carefully around him and continued. Sanja kept saying, the whole time: "Drive carefully! Please, drive carefully!" She thinks there's something wrong with my concentration. And she's probably right. When the bikers had disappeared from my rearview mirror, she said: "The woman on the motorbike wasn't wearing a helmet." (That's against the law in the States.) She's become very perceptive.

This morning I'm driving to work, the roads are empty, but at the exit for the Pentagon I'm joined by a group of bikers. I drive with them escorting me, which is quite an unusual situation. Alone on the road with the bikers, each one with the American flag sewn onto the back of his jacket or jeans. In Rosslyn, they turn onto Route 66, toward the airport, while I carry on over Key Bridge, my Taurus is the only car on the bridge, its electrics are faulty, on the dashboard the green digital numbers say that it is 9:45 in the morning, while my phone says 7:25. I enter Georgetown, go down into the garage, where there are a few cars. I emerge from underground back into a cloudy morning. The board under the inscription BLUES ALLEY is not displaying the usual name of a musician, which means that there's no concert in the jazz club tonight. I go into our building, darkness, there's no one around. I switch on the computers and hurry to check our monthly timetable because I believe that I'll find the answer there. And there it is: today's a holiday, Memorial Day, I should have remembered that as I drove with the bikers. I would have known if I'd taken notice of the news over the weekend. But I simply routinely repeat actions in which my consciousness participates only superficially. My reality is her paralyzed arm. Time is measured by the short intervals between her medications. I'm so close to her that forgetfulness is settling into me like a narcotic.

I have tamed the alarm by no longer locking the car door. I've discovered that for some reason unlocking the door confuses it. The car doesn't recognize my key, so it thinks I'm a thief and that's why the alarm goes off. We got the Taurus as a gift from Kendra a year ago. When she offered us her old car, I was hesitant, because I didn't like the look of it. I remembered that, at the turn of the century, the American auto industry began to be dominated by a fairly unappealing design, all vehicles were a bit egg-shaped, while the Ford Taurus, with its rounded and curved parts, stood out particularly for its ugliness. Had anyone then offered me a new one, I would certainly not have taken it. I wouldn't now, either, in all probability, but we needed a car because we'd moved to a building some distance from a Metro station, so that on my way to work I would have had to change my means of transport three times. I accepted the gift. Otherwise, I always give my cars names, and when Sanja asked me: "What's it called?" I said, with a smile: "Corto Maltese!" But I think that I only really accepted the car after she became ill, because everything would really have been much harder without transport. This morning we went to buy fruit. On our way back we went down to the shop's garage in the elevator, with our bags of blackcurrants and strawberries. When the door opened, among a dozen nondescript cars of various colors I caught sight of our Taurus. And it looked good! Among all the others, it looked to me convincingly better-looking.

My interest in memory loss has already existed a long time, and last year, after a routine visit to the doctor, my cardiologist explained that forgetfulness is one of the side effects of the medication I've been taking for years now. Soon after that, I went to Arizona to see, twenty years on, our first American address in Phoenix. And I wrote a diary during that journey in which I tried to discover the extent of my forgetting. Fear of forgetting had started to become an obsession with me some time ago, so this loss of Sanja's is more than pure coincidence. The question I kept asking myself in the solitude of the hospital room was: Does our obsessive preoccupation with specific topics mean that we influence events ourselves, or do we unconsciously recall our near future, so that the memory expresses a deeper interest in problems we have yet to encounter? Did I influence what happened to Sanja, or have I been remembering it for some time already as an event that had yet to come?

Here's another brief memory in connection with our first address as a contribution to the theme of forgetting. Some time ago Harun wrote the screenplay for a film that opened with a violent war scene in which a girl was injured and her man killed. The consequence of her injury was amnesia. She did not remember anything. The Red Cross discovered that her husband was in fact still alive, because they found his name and a new address on their lists. She went there, although she had already forgotten everything connected with him, she couldn't even remember what he looked like. The man she was going to meet was in fact the man who had killed her husband and then used his personal documents to leave the country under his false identity. And the place of their meeting was a community in Phoenix, that first American address of ours.

When Harun and I turned up last year in front of "our" apartment in Phoenix, nothing happened, not a single sign that the place recognized us. Not only people, but places too can experience amnesia.

I had decided to take Sanja to Blues Alley on Friday, to a concert by Arturo Sandoval, I thought it was time for us to begin participating in events, so that she'd have things to remember. But it was too ambitious a plan. This morning (it's Friday) she woke with a bad pain in her right arm, tired and out of sorts, and she doesn't want to leave the house. After work, I go out the back door into Blues Alley, it's raining, on and off, and in front of the bar Arturo Sandoval is standing, alone and lost in thought, in a blue linen jacket, he's holding a *cohiba* between his fingers, occasionally glancing at the sky and puffing out thick smoke. I want to talk to him, but I can't think what to say, so I walk past him, continue along Avenue Wisconsin, and go down into the underground garage. I have two tickets for the concert in my pocket, I check that I haven't lost them along the way, I'm still hoping that the pain in her arm will have eased.

Since her stroke, her perception has sharpened, she sees the anomalies or correctness around her more clearly, the logic and illogicality of phenomena. I brought her cherries.

"Americans don't make a substantive distinction between sweet and sour cherries, they're all 'cherries' to them. Whereas we have *višnja*, Morello cherry, and *trešnja*, sweet cherry. Did you have any little girls in your school called Višnja? We had several in my school. But not a single Trešnja. We have an expression: 'If the *višnja* was like the *trešnja*,' implying that the latter was better and nicer than the former, and yet little girls were named after the sour cherry, not the sweet. That must be because of the energy of the words, because, as far as

I'm concerned, a watermelon, *lubenica*, is tastier than either kind of cherry, but it seems unnatural to call a girl Lubenica. I don't like my own name, Sanja, I never accepted it, it's not me. I'd prefer to be called Višnja. Or Dunja (quince). Of all the fruits, the nicest girl's name is Dunja. You come across Malina (raspberry), but you'd never find a girl called Kupina (blackberry). And, now, think about it, in our language not a single fruit or plant is masculine. Apart from *jasen* (aspen), if the name Jasenko comes from *jasen*. No, I tell a lie! There's also Jasmin, after the flower. And maybe there is some other name that comes from a plant, which I've forgotten, since the stroke . . . There's the girl's name Jelka (fir tree), but there isn't a single man called Bor (pine), although that would be a good name."

We buy cherries every other day. Even in our childhood they weren't this tasty. This is the year of the cherry.

"As a matter of interest, where did you get your name?"

"From my cousin, Semezdin. In April 1992, my uncle Rizo, Semezdin's father, phoned me in Sarajevo from Tuzla and said: 'You write for the papers . . . You should know that everything you write will one day be used against you,' In short, he was asking me to be careful what I said, because in a war people can die because of the wrong word. 'Be careful!' he repeated several times. That was an unusual conversation at the beginning of the war. And at the end I asked him about the origin of my name. It's after a Circassian, he said. A Circassian who lived in Bijeljina, in northeast Bosnia. He was a musician and a convivial man, his forebears had been exiled by the Russians from the eastern shore of the Black Sea, from a place called Semez. So, the name came from the Circassian's nostalgia for the place of his birth. I like this little theory about the name, and I'd like to believe it, but I haven't been able to find any reference in books to a place of that name on the shore of the Black Sea, so I have to take my uncle's explanation with a pinch of salt."

She watches the same film every day. Her taste for repetition is nothing new, that's how she's been since the late 1980s, when she began reading just one book, Thomas Mann's *The Magic Mountain.* Over the last decade, she has largely watched *Pride and Prejudice*, in all its film versions. She explained frankly: she is drawn to a world that exists only in costume drama. "I'm only interested in a world where there are no telephone poles."

"What are you going to do today?"

"I'll watch my film . . . Don't laugh. I think that's a virtue. People easily lose interest in things, they treat each other like novelties and quickly get bored with them. I'm devoted to my film. I'm true to my choices."

The film she watches obsessively is about a pair of ice skaters, because the cold in the images of snow and ice appeals to her, because as a result of the stroke, the right side of her body, especially her right arm, is prone to waves of heat. And whenever she watches it in her room, the film functions as air-conditioning.

"It's as though I'm dreaming everything I see . . ." That's always her first sentence when we come outside. "I'm not sure whether what I'm seeing is really real. Or am I imagining it? I keep thinking this is a dream, that I'll wake up and everything will be as it was before." She doesn't remember. She knows that she's had a stroke, because she keeps being told, and she knows because of the aftereffects (pressure in the right side of her body). Nevertheless, she has trouble believing that it really happened to her, because she doesn't remember the event itself. She keeps experiencing that state when we wake in the morning and try in vain to recall a dream of the night before. Or the other way around, as though everything is a dream from which she will wake at any moment. As though she's imprisoned in someone else's dream.

Last Saturday, at the swimming pool, I was sitting at a table under a sunshade. Sanja was in the water; I heard her voice and thought she was calling me. I sat up straight, came out of the shade, and saw her arguing with a swimmer who was saying: "This is a swimming pool!"

"Yes, it is, but it's not just yours!"

And I went over to the edge of the pool: "What's going on?" "Nothing," she says. "This man splashes too much when he's swimming."

I lowered myself carefully into the water, although I didn't really feel like swimming. The man straightened up, pushed his swimming goggles onto the top of his head, and looked at me, and I was close enough to see on his shoulder the tattoo of a hand with a raised middle finger. A rebellious message to the world. The tattoo explained his arrogant attitude to Sanja as well. He was showing the whole world, including me as I swam toward him, a tattooed middle finger. An old-fashioned tattoo the color of pale indigo is in fact a threatening sign drawn on the skin with a needle. I hadn't quite reached him when he turned and slowly waddled off to the edge of the pool, leaped energetically out, sprinkling water all around him, and went back to his recliner. "Look at him! Running away with his tail between his legs," she says. But I had gone simply to calm her and to protect her with my body from the water others splashed about. She watched him victoriously as he left, and that flattered my male pride.

And this evening, as we crossed the parking lot, a couple passed us. Tanned, they were smoking as they left the pool. He was the young man with the tattoo of a hand showing its middle finger to the world. The slight aroma of tobacco hung in the air as they went. Sanja stopped, turned, and watched them walk away. She closed her eyes, trying to remember, or simply to smell the smoke in the air. Then she came to and followed me.

She's a real little girl! We're at the swimming pool, she's lying on her front on a recliner, watching a column of ants moving along the crack between two cement blocks, she has blocked their passage with a finger and is waiting to see whether they'll start climbing up her hand. But the ants make a detour in an arc around her finger. And I say: "You know, Jules Renard has a very short story about ants, shall I tell you it?" "Go on." "He says that every ant looks like the figure 3. And how many there are! 3 3 3 3 3 3 3 3 3 3 3 3 3 3 3 3 3 3 . . . to infinity . . ." She says nothing. And I don't know whether she likes my version of Renard's story. She's usually talkative, but sometimes (and ever more frequently) she closes herself up completely and then there's no way I can get her to speak.

After my heart attack (November 2010), the doctor said I had "survived this time," but if I had to come to him again, I wouldn't leave the hospital. He explained that there were five things I must give up, counting them all out on the fingers of his left hand: 1. cigarettes, 2. cigarettes, 3. cigarettes, 4. cigarettes, 5. cigarettes. Sanja took his explanation literally, and I had no choice, I had to stop smoking. Four years later, at Ivica Puljić's apartment, I lit a cigarette on the balcony and puffed a bit, it was a delightful, cheerful gathering, with a lot of dear and interesting people, but then Sanja caught sight of me in a cloud of smoke and went berserk, shouting at me and bursting into tears. At midnight she rushed outside and I followed her, and our friends were left in shock. In the morning they called to apologize, as though they were to blame for my lighting up.

Last month, Obama was in Cuba, and my colleagues from work went to Cuba to report on the historic visit of the American president. When they were preparing for the journey, H. asked what they should bring me, and I said a *cohiba*. I said it without thinking, more from a need to give her an impossible task, because Cuban cigars could still not be brought across the American border. But, at some risk, traveling in the group of journalists accompanying Obama, H. brought over a wooden box of twenty-five *cohiba*s. I don't know whose pleasure was greater, mine when I was given the gift or hers because she had been able to smuggle the cigars for me. When I came home with the box, Sanja dug in her heels, what's this, was I going to start smoking again? Of course not, these are cigars, you just puff on them, you don't inhale and they aren't dangerous. Out of the question! And I said: Okay, the box is just for a decoration on the table, I'll give the cigars to friends, until they're all gone. Nevertheless, she kept a close eye on the box, secretly opening it and counting the cigars in it, while I would take one in the morning in

a little ziplock bag, justifying myself by saying it was a gift for
Ivica or Asim or Santiago; at the end of the day, she would
sniff me to check whether I smelled of tobacco. Every time I use the word *puff*, I think of Mirko Kovač.
He never smoked, he told me, he simply didn't like the smell
of tobacco smoke. But once, in a Moscow hotel, his friend, a
film director, opened a box of cigars in front of him that were
specially made in Cuba for the Yugoslav president. There was
a gold ring round each cigar, with TITO inscribed on it. "I had
to try one, to see what a cigar called TITO tasted like! But I
didn't know that cigars should be puffed, that their smoke
should not be inhaled. I took three drags and passed out."

Ever since we came back from the hospital, she has been
glancing suspiciously at the wooden box, unable to remember how the Cuban cigars came to be on my desk. Nor does
she remember her fears. She opened the box and established
that the remaining cigars were drying in the air of the room
and said: "Maybe we should put a couple of cabbage leaves
in the box . . . ?" (In our country dry tobacco used to be "re-
freshed" with a green cabbage leaf.)

I am reminded of 4 September 2012, when I was in Zagreb
and met up with Kovač, who was unwell and was supposed
to go the next day for some hospital tests. Over dinner in
a restaurant, he tried out a new topic on his companions.
He spoke about his experience of being ill and of hospitals,

because his "new reality" had produced quite unique images that he would like to describe. "In the hospital," he said, "in the oncology department I watched two amorous patients, a man and a woman, kissing passionately, while their metal oxygen bottles knocked into each other, clanging . . ."

She's always sad when she remembers her youth. Today, we were on our way to a restaurant and the radio was playing a song from the 1980s ("Every Breath You Take") and she burst into tears. When she calmed down, she said: "Were gramophone records at home called *sound carriers?*" She remembers language.

We live a lonely life, we have few friends here, they can be counted on the fingers of one hand. They sometimes come to see us. Today her American friend Kendra came out of the elevator at the same moment as I opened the door of our apartment to wait for her, but the distance between us was great, it's a long way from the elevator to our door, the corridor is straight and infinite, I waved to her, but she gave no sign that she'd seen me. That's our corridor. I was too far away for her to see me, she walked for a long time from the elevator to our door, and when she was quite close I saw that she was carrying flowers in a small pot, very elegant white calla lilies.

Sanja doesn't like being given flowers that aren't in pots.

She calls flowers that have had their stems cut before being put into a vase "ripped." Dead flowers. When she gives flowers, they're always in a pot, with their roots in soil and instructions for watering them. That's how it's always been, as long as I've known her. "It's impolite to give dead flowers to sick people. Imagine expressing care, or love, or friendship by giving one another dead birds!"

In the building opposite us there are three young Arab men on the balcony. This is the third night that they've been carousing until morning. They have two hookahs on the table in front of them, they talk loudly, laughing and singing. They must just have arrived in this country and don't know nighttime rules, there's no loud singing on balconies here. I was listening not to them, but to Sanja's breathing; if they woke her, I was thinking of calling the police. Although I hoped someone else would do that for me, because when the police came and took their names, they would no doubt arrest them as terrorists. And then this evening I heard a police car under their balcony and now they've settled down. I've just been watching them through the window: bare to the waist, they smoke and converse quite quietly, maybe they sing in a whisper, while their gestures suggest that they're rappers . . .

There's always an excess of bread in the house, she makes it into croutons for my salad, but there's still more than we need. That's because of our wartime hunger. There has to be enough food in the house, just in case. When I take the left-over bread toward the rubbish bin, she objects: "You mustn't throw bread away!" She never throws it away, she crumbles it and gives it to the birds. And now I'm tossing them crumbs instead of her. This evening, I say, I didn't see any birds gathering to eat them, just squirrels and dogs being walked by their owners. And she says: "That's fine, all animals are birds when they eat crumbs."

She sleeps, and when she wakes, she gets up and goes to the fridge. This hunger dates from her hospital days. And it already shows on her body, she's put on weight. I made a short video lasting ten seconds on my phone, I showed it to her cautiously and she waved me away: "Cameras add eight kilos." When was the last time I heard that! People used to say it in the 1960s and '70s, when the only cameras were for television. Through them, the human body weighed eight kilos more than in reality, I don't know according to what scales. If I suggest she's eating something she shouldn't, it distresses her, and she says: "You're torturing me with hunger." And then I haven't the heart . . .

"Do you remember when you fed the birds at the pond in the garden of the building where you worked?"

"Yes, but I didn't know they were migratory birds. They got fat and they couldn't fly south."

✦

She refuses to go out and constantly looks for an excuse to go back to bed. "It's time to sleep. I've always been interested in that state of hibernation when you are neither alive nor dead. Then the brain switches off and rests. The brain is a creature that lives in us. I know that's not biologically correct, but I find it interesting to think like that. And sleeping is always agreeable. Sometimes it isn't, because of nightmares, but far more often it is, because if that weren't the case we'd probably have great resistance to abandoning ourselves to a state in which our consciousness is switched off, and we're closest to death. If dying was the same as falling asleep, perhaps people would be nicer to each other and there would be fewer problems in our lives. Because life could be good and simple if people didn't complicate it for each other. And the number of heart attacks and strokes would diminish . . ."

We spend a lot of time remembering the past, that's how we check how much of everything we've forgotten. We keep making lists, remembering important books, songs, or films. "I remember that, before New Year's, we went to a little cinema to see *Pride and Prejudice*. It was sunny when we went in, and when we came out it was snowing!" I remember that snow as well.

Some ten years have passed since then.

We have plenty of time, so that every day we revive our

memories of the same events. And there always comes a moment when she asks: "Tell me which of our acquaintances
has died." I don't like that question, because I know how up-
setting my answers will be, many of those closest to us have
died in recent years. Every day I alter my replies, so as to
make them less stressful, but that doesn't help much. Over
and over again, with the same intensity, she hears the news of
the same death. I'm afraid that this multiplication of events,
like the reflections of the human body in two mirrors placed
opposite each other, will be completely devastating for her.
Every day, as though for the first time, she learns the news of
the death of other people. I thought of stopping mentioning
the dead. But if I start concealing the past, she won't forgive
me when she does eventually remember everything. And I
believe that she will emerge from her forgetfulness, as one
emerges from a dark cinema into the light of a lively city
street.

"We've both had *attacks*," she says. "Harun is a child with
attacked parents."

On Saturday, we were at the swimming pool, lying on recliners and blinking in the shade of a small tree. When the wind
bends the branches, they come close to our faces. We look up
into the canopy with its small green leaves, the sun at times
flashing through them. We lie there. The leaves rustle, the

water murmurs. And then she says: "I've always liked looking at the sun through branches like this. When I was in nursery school, there were acacia trees in the garden. Now it's as though I was in fact looking through the leaves of those acacias. What's this tree called?"

"I don't know."

"When we were children we used to eat the blossom."

I took a short video on my phone of the living leaves above us, lasting about twenty seconds, and then slowly moved the phone toward her, I took her face briefly, three or four seconds, and stopped. Then I showed her the video. As far as we could see it on the telephone in the reflected daylight, the little film seemed nice. When we got home and I looked at it carefully, I had stopped recording at the moment when she turned her face to look at me. Oh, that look haunts me now. Such an expression of bliss, reconciliation, and absence of vanity, such a lack of interest in posing and withdrawal from everything . . . Melancholy, but beautiful! We stayed at the pool for two hours and she was glad we were there, even though the water was cold; she had gone to the edge of the pool with great enthusiasm, but after dipping her toe into the water, she gave up on the idea of swimming. Earlier, too, when we were crossing the parking lot in front of our building on the way to the pool, she was quite happy: "I feel more natural in the water. Water is my closest element. Maybe some forebear of mine was a mermaid!" I thought she was happy. But then the cold lens of the telephone camera revealed the look in her eyes . . . How could one console a person with such a look?

Sometimes, when she's cheerful like today, she says that her forgetfulness is not a problem, or that it is a lesser problem than the pressure she feels in her right arm.

"I don't think there have been such important events in my life that I should remember them. Besides, we don't even remember our birth, and that ought to be one of the most crucial events. If only my arm would stop hurting. Forgetting doesn't hurt . . ."

Questions we repeat every morning. "What day is it today?" "Which year?" "What month is this?" Outside the wind says Juuuuuuuune.

She opens up pages on the internet randomly researching what she's forgotten and what she still remembers. She tires quickly because of problems with her sight; sometimes what she reads disturbs her, and sometimes she's pleased with what she finds. In an online dictionary she found the word *labrnja*, laughing at the sound of the word itself and its meaning. *Labrnja*: the space for the teeth. "In Bosnia men used to tell women to 'shut their *labrnja*!' Imagine that: shut the space for your teeth!"

Otherwise, recently she has tended to divide the world into men's and women's sections, and she defends her gender. She was looking at some photographs from the end of the nineteenth or early twentieth century and said: "This isn't female one-upmanship, but look for yourself at male history! Just look at the models of beards and mustaches. How much time has passed since the mustache of Franz Jozef was in fashion? An emperor, with something like this on his face (she taps the screen of her iPad), sideburns and mustache joined together in an unsuccessful birds' nest! It would be a mercy to shave it off." (She used the expression *štucovati*, otherwise a word we had taken from the German *stutzen*, meaning "cut very short," that had reached us with the emperor Franz Jozef.) "We should go through time, since the beginning of the world, cutting all beards and mustaches very short."

At the swimming pool. There's a squirrel in the tree above our recliners. We watch it, and it seems to me that it's looking at us, too. And Sanja says: "It's possible that the molecules of water in that squirrel were once in the body of Leonardo da Vinci!"

She said she fancied pomegranate seeds. I went to the commercial center and bought six large pomegranates. When I brought them home, she said: "That's too many. Who could eat all those? And they're already overripe . . ." She didn't go near them for two days, but today she cut one open. How easily the rind broke! That Saturday it was sunny in our room, and the bright sun illuminated the perfectly red seeds in the freshly opened fruit. "Oh, God was pretty inspired when he created the pomegranate. So, he had a good day!" She scooped out the seeds and went on: "It's completely illogical for God to be male, since males don't give birth. Religion is proof that there's a lie at the heart of the male imagination. The pomegranate could only have been invented by an architect of the female gender. An architectess."

She talked and talked. I broke in, in the brief pauses between her sentences, repeating: "I know, I know."

And she said: "I know you know, but I have to say something."

Today she's teaching me to cook. We bump into each other by the cooker, fight over the space that used to be exclusively hers, and then a little bit mine. She says: "It's only in *sogan dolma* that onion is treated with some dignity. Mostly it is chopped into a dish and so becomes an important ingredient. It's only in *sogan dolma* that the whole architecture of the dish is based on it, on its form . . ." I follow her instructions obediently. She looks at those picturesque glass containers she has been filling with herbs and spices, whose aromas she is now rediscovering. She holds a dry, gray-green leaf on her open palm and, as though she were remembering everything, says: "I always liked food that included a bay leaf . . ."

She starts cooking. She's making butter biscuits. She's got flour even on her socks.

I took food she had prepared for me to work, mostly salads, but she'd never cut the vegetables completely, so that they didn't lose their freshness, I had to do that later, and so along with the container of food she added a knife to the bag, metal, but colored orange, so that at first glance it appears to be plastic. It's very sharp. Last year I traveled to Boston, and at the airport I passed through the body scanner, I turned around to wait for my luggage and then on the screen in front of the security officer I saw the inside of my hand baggage and in it my knife! Several officers in blue shirts came running up to me, and I said: "That's for salad!" They explained agreeably that I couldn't get onto the plane with that object, so I had two options: to throw the knife into the rubbish bin, or to post it to my home address. They gave me a FedEx cardboard envelope, I filled in everything I had to, put the knife in the envelope, stuck it down, and handed it to the agreeable official. From the plane I phoned Sanja to tell her what had happened, and she said: "It's a good thing you didn't end up in jail!" And she said we shouldn't open the envelope when it arrived. We should keep it closed as an art object or a time capsule.

✦

The day before I brought her back from the hospital, I visited the apartment to prepare the rooms for her arrival: I washed, dusted, and vacuumed. Behind the sofa I saw a miniature spider, a spiderling, so small that it wouldn't have been able to survive my touch. I left it to weave its slender threads. Two weeks have passed since then, Sanja has just woken up on the sofa and there's the red trace of a spider bite on her forehead! She's still allergic to them. And that's the rule in our relationship. Everything that occurs is, after all, my fault.

No one visits us anymore. I hadn't thought about that before, but it's clear to me now: people are afraid of a sick person.

One of her most frequent questions: "How did Harun take all of this?" I tell her that her son was here for ten days in April. I'm used to her question, I have a prepared answer that always surprises her because she has forgotten everything, and then she repeats the same question: "And did he hug me when he came?" She asks this with such seriousness and waits for my answer with such concentration, as though a hug were a precise test of a son's love.

Our son and his photographs. When we moved into this apartment, she chose four of his photos and had them framed. I had my own suggestions, but she immediately rejected them, because their subjects "didn't bring healthy energy into the room." For instance, my favorite photograph of Harun's is of a girl in red, beside a large fire. She hesitated, but then confessed that she didn't want to "hang a fire" on the wall of our room. Opposite our bed is a photograph of a girl sitting on the edge of a tall building, her bare feet hang in the air, and below her is Route 66 and a green traffic sign displaying the turnings for Pentagon City, Crystal City, and Alexandria. The river intersects with the road, you can see all the bridges apart from Key Bridge, and in the distance the tower of the airport (DCA). For the last twenty years, this is the way I have driven to work. How often have I turned at this very crossroads toward Alexandria! How often have I crossed each of these bridges, at all hours of the day and in all seasons. No space in the world is so imprinted in my body as this panorama, which I see, spread out, from my bed. Earlier, when I looked at the photograph, I used to pay attention to the depth of the image and the familiar roads, but now I'm disturbed by the girl sitting on the edge of the high building in Rosslyn. Her face is covered with her hair. She's wearing a dress (a wedding dress?) that is probably white, but because of the morning (or evening?) light, its material has a violet tinge. I hadn't thought of this till now, but that girl could have been Sanja in her late twenties or early thirties. It's quite possible that she identified with her, and that's why she chose this photograph and put it in an important place, so that she sees it every day before she drifts off to sleep. She didn't want to hang up the picture of the girl beside the fire (for fear of its dubious "energy" in the room), but she chose a girl sitting on the rim of an abyss. What was it she had relinquished?

"I don't feel like going back to my job. I studied philosophy, but it didn't get me anywhere. I did tedious, bureaucratic work. Now I'd like to change my profession."

"What would you like to do now?"

"I'd like to look after dragons. I know dragons don't exist, but one can be a keeper of creatures from stories. They, too, need protection."

After a visit to the doctor, on our way home we stopped at the Starbucks at Bailey's Crossroads. We used to go there sometimes, in the days when we lived near the café, which is frequented mostly by immigrants from Africa. I watched her stop in front of the door of the women's toilet, which was, it turned out, locked, so she waited patiently. Sanja always does this: first she goes to wash her hands, like a religious ritual. After a minute or two, the door opened and then I saw a girl coming out, she could have been nineteen or twenty; immediately after her, a young man emerged as well. It's not exactly a frequent phenomenon here, in puritan America, to see a man coming out of a space intended only for women. Sanja turned to me, spread her hands, and smiled. There was a smile on the face of the girl as well, but it expressed her embarrassment, in fact shame, because she'd been caught in an act that wasn't publicly approved, and as though she felt a need to hide, she went over to the newspaper stand and stared at the photograph on the front page of *The New York Times*; the young man followed her and they quickly slipped out of the café. The lovers were young Arabs (the girl's face was framed in a gray silk scarf).

After that, we drank our coffee, laughing, and didn't mention the event that had caused this gaiety. "It's all going to be all right," I said. Everything will be good. And from time to time I turned toward the newspaper stand and looked at the photograph on the front page of *The New York Times*.

It was a photo of a rickety bridge made of old rough boards, in a gentle arc over a stream, the tributary of a river or sea with tropical marsh plants growing beside it. In the foreground sits a three-year-old girl in a light gray sleeveless top and trousers of the same color, her feet are apart, but her knees touch, so that her whole little child's body forms the shape of an X. Her little fingers are fiddling with a small orange flower, which she's looking at as though she were hiding and she's clearly uncomfortable about being photographed. The bridge leads to a house without a door, and a white cat with black ears and a black tail (its back turned to the camera lens) has stopped in the middle of the little bridge and turned to look at the child. There's something inconsolable in the pose of the little girl and in the cat's turning. (The caption under the photo is *Resettling the First American "Climate Refugees."*)

She has begun to read, she says she must inform herself about world events, but her problems with her sight slow her down; she can't stay long at the computer screen, and she's irritable. She reads the news on the internet, then says: "It says *in the paper . . .*"

Until this evening I didn't know that she really is keeping up with the daily news. We had just watched a film (*The Magic of Ordinary Days*, Hallmark's love story from the Second World War) in which there are images of a concentration camp, the prisoners are Japanese, in fact people born here, so Americans, most of them had never seen Japan, and their only "sin" was their ethnic origin. And, as we watched those scenes, she said: "If Trump wins the election, they'll set up camps for Muslims here!"

We are accompanied by what is perhaps an unfounded fear. In the autumn and winter of 2001, Muslims here were suspected, followed, and arrested. Once, we were coming back from shopping and saw several police cars in front of the entrance to our building, their doors open, and we heard the crackling noises of their police walkie-talkies, and she said: "They've come for us!" We stood on the opposite side of the road, with plastic bags in our hands as dusk fell, watching the red revolving lights floating above the police cars, and she said: "They've come for us!"

She says she slept badly last night, because a "talkative family of cicadas" had moved in under our window. ("Are cicadas, too, illegal immigrants in this country?")

The hospital invoices are arriving. At the end of the day, I went down to our mailbox on the ground floor. On my way back, I returned along the lengthy corridor and heard footsteps behind me. I turned around, but there was no one there. I went on walking and listening to the sounds of my own footsteps, convinced that a moment before I had perhaps heard myself, my own trudging, and mistakenly believed that someone was following me. But then the footsteps started again, along with muffled panting, as though I were being followed by someone accompanied by a dog; I turn around, there's no one, just the empty corridor as far as the eye can see. In our building there are more dogs than people. As far as noise goes, this building is a real zoo. I had just unlocked the door and entered our apartment. The footsteps stopped. I'd like to believe I'm imagining the sounds because of my physical and mental exhaustion. ("Who is the third who always walks beside you?" T. S. Eliot.)

◆

"I can't take it anymore, I'm tired, I just want to go and be with my grandmas and grandpas, with Mensur and Muzafa, with Ibrahim and Fikreta!" (Those are the names of our dead . . .) This isn't the ordinary loneliness of one who has been left with no collocutor or without the closeness of another person, another body, it isn't the isolation of Robinson Crusoe. It is, I fear, the isolation in which the dead are more real than the living.

I am gradually discovering that her forgetting is deeper and that her memory is fairly selective. It seems to me that she has forgotten everything apart from her fears.

When we left the hospital, I had hoped that, as soon as she was surrounded by familiar objects, she'd start to remember. In addition, I was absolutely sure that she'd now begin to recall new events, and that this would begin to build her new memory. When she's surrounded by familiar faces, I thought, we'll conquer her forgetfulness. But that didn't happen. Familiar faces no longer calm her. "They remember me while I was in hospital, but I don't remember that. Everyone else now knows more about my life than I do. I'm a stranger to myself. I'm Camus's Outsider."

It's clear that the state of her right arm has gotten worse, the sensitivity of her hand has been reduced so that she often burns herself on the gas flame when she's cooking, or she cuts herself, which is a serious problem, because she's taking blood thinners, which make the healing process more difficult. Today I told her: "It's hard to stop our bleeding." I talk about her in the plural; instead of saying *she*, I say *we*. I have identified myself with her state. Yesterday I bought two boxes of Band-Aids of various sizes. The pressure in her arm is sometimes so powerful that she gives up on everything. My care, even my presence in the same room now bother her. I go to my desk, but she follows me almost immediately, because she thinks I'm angry, and asks: "Would you like me to make you some tea?" And that shatters me.

Earlier ("before the stroke"), she defended her right to solitude, she'd go to the bedroom after dinner and watch her films on her own. When I chided her for that, she'd say she had a "cat's nature," solitary . . . But now she's sociable, if I go away, if I'm at my desk, writing, she invents little diversions to encourage me to talk. She's forgotten many events from the past, now she's discovering the world all over again and showing a child's curiosity about it.

"May I ask you something?"

"Of course."

"What do you think about Jesus?"

That's the kind of unexpected question she starts a conversation with.

She asks: "What do you think about butterflies? I think

they're beautiful, but they frighten me when I see them up close . . ."

She's become highly entertaining company.

A hot day, extremely humid. We set off to buy coffee filters. It's getting dark, the heat isn't easing. And before we parted company in the parking lot, because I'm irritable in this heat, she said: "You go and sniff books, do something for your soul!" She went to get the filters, while I went into a bookshop and bought a book. Jean-Dominique Bauby, *The Diving Bell and the Butterfly*, it was made into a fine film, I saw it about ten years ago, and the time has come now for me to read it. It's about a man who's paralyzed, after experiencing "a massive stroke."

There was no sign of Sanja, so I went to help her with the shopping. I caught sight of her in the fruit section. I keep reliving the moment of our *meeting*. I remember, it was thirty years ago now, I was looking out the window of my student room at number 2 Franje Račkog and—there she was!—she was turning out of Vilsonovo Šetalište toward the window I was looking out of, her hair was wet from bathing . . . It must be that serotonin or some other neurotransmitter in my brain is automatically activated the instant I see her, because then my whole state changes for the better. I watched her secretly for a few minutes choosing fruit. The year when I had my heart attack, the grapes were very good, this year it's cherries that are particularly delicious. Every year is different. I watch her smelling the peaches. But the fruit we buy today has no aroma.

The insurance company that is obliged to pay her sick leave is trying to free itself from that obligation. Since she had her stroke, the people who run the company where Sanja worked for eighteen years in the department dealing with the protection of refugees have not called once to ask how she is. Every time I call the insurance company, the person who answers the phone says that a certain Donna Pellegrini is working on "Sanja's case" and will contact us and let us know about everything. Three weeks have passed, and Donna Pellegrini has not called. And so, in our world, Donna Pellegrini is the most important and therefore the most frequently mentioned person, although it is perfectly possible that she is an invented, nonexistent figure.

A quiet afternoon at work. With the volume low, I'm recording the speech of the Republican candidate Donald Trump, when I feel something warm on the back of my neck. I turn around and behind me is an ash-colored pit bull breathing heavily, one of those dogs with tiny eyes with small pupils, looking threateningly at me and growling, or I may have imagined the growling in my alarm. Fortunately, a woman soon appeared in the doorway, calling to the dog as though she were addressing a two-year-old. She apologized for taking it away from me. Exactly that: She apologized for depriving me of its company, convinced I was enjoying it. People here really like dogs. In the relationship between the dog, its owner, and me, I was actually the one at fault. The pit bull was not to blame for alarming me. My resistance to dogs is an absence of empathy, while dog owners cannot see beyond their emotional system; they expect the rest of the world to relate to their pets with the same fondness they do, because in the world of a person who loves, the only criterion is love.

Refugees have two worlds, the one they have left and the one where they are now. The antagonism of the two worlds is the essence of exile. That duality is carried over into language: the first language is the mother tongue, the other the language of the new surroundings. After a stroke, a person may forget their language, or one of them, or they may begin speaking a quite different language, with which they had not previously been in contact. Sanja's languages are all present and correct, and she has no difficulty in moving from one to the other, in that sense nothing has changed. But the atlas of her world is confused. She sometimes wakes convinced she is in Sarajevo. She says: "I must go to work."

"OK, if you go out of our door now, how will you get to work?"

"I go down in the elevator, come out of the building,

cross the road, then over the big parking lot, I go to the underground, take it first to the left, then we make a circle to Čengić Vila ...”

“This is Washington, there’s no Čengić Vila here ...”

She’s confused because of her own nightmare, but then she redeems herself, charmingly: “How shameful! What kind of town is this with no Čengić Vila?”

The medication that is meant to reduce her pain and depression is called Lyrica. *This is the way the world ends.* By a word changing its meaning.

We were told that the windows would be cleaned at the end of last week. A workman came on Tuesday and removed the protective meshes that stop tiny creatures coming in when the windows are open. But the cleaners have postponed their part of the work for a week. Today it’s Saturday, and because everything was open, a sparrow came in through one of our windows, it flew about frantically and then did manage to find a way out through a different window. It all happened quickly. The air that the little bird had swirled about in the room turned the page of the book I was just reading.

I make notes in haste, along the way, in the car, in the elevator, in bed, just woken from sleep, because if I don’t record things straightaway, I will certainly forget them. But if it weren’t for this notetaking, if there were no moments when I turn into myself, I feel I would exist less, or I would forget myself.

Each of these moments exists in a perpetual present. But, nevertheless, every word of this diary will be forgotten. This book will no longer exist, nor will there be anyone who remembers her.

There are *nows*, says Julian Barbour, there are various *nows* and all those *nows* exist simultaneously, as different possibilities. And that's all. No one and nothing travels from one *now* into the next *now*. We pass, but time does not.

Life is the flight of a sparrow that flutters in through one window and flies out another.

Fifteen years ago, it was raining. A taxi driver was taking us to the fish market, because you wanted to see the restaurant that features in one scene of the film *Sleepless in Seattle*. But when we reached the restaurant, you were disappointed. In the film it was a more attractive and better-lit place, while we entered a small, dusty bistro. The difference between the fictional and nonfictional is not the same as the difference between the real and the illusory. In the case of this concrete restaurant, it's a real place, used in the past for the needs of a fictitious film story. "Everything looks better in a film!" you said, with a note of regret in your voice. When we're young, we want our love story to be unique. It would have been better if you hadn't met me, for our relationship contained no material for romantic comedy. It's always better in a film, there's no smell of fish slowly thawing on the stalls of the great Market. Life stinks.

"Sem Mehmedinovik! The man who has a rubbish bin in his car!" That's how my friend Santiago, the cheery Spaniard, introduced me today.

But that's because of Sanja's need to put everything around her in order. There mustn't be any rubbish on the floor. That's why we have a rubbish bin in our old Ford Taurus.

She listens to music so as to remember her youth, on the whole songs from the late 1960s and '70s (mostly Crosby, Stills, Nash & Young). And she says: "Woodstock, how magical that sounded in the Balkans! But Woodstock is a store for wood! How provincial we were! Why, even those who knew what the word *Woodstock* meant would not be moved. It does sound mighty in English! It could not be an ordinary wood store. And if it was to do with trees, they would have been some special American trees, and not our beech or our common oak . . ."

Today we went for a doctor's examination. The doctor (a neurologist), said several times that it was a serious question whether our medical insurance could cover the costs of the memory test (this was, allegedly, an expensive examination to determine the extent of forgetfulness). She repeated that it was "a serious question" three times, and then Sanja lost patience and said that it couldn't possibly be a serious question. "Why does Something exist, and not Nothing? That's a serious question!" she said.

And, it seemed to me, time had stood still. It has been two months since Renata cut her hair, but her hair doesn't seem to be growing.

The only items of value in our apartment are books. And this bookshelf, handmade, the work of an American sculptor. It's made of light wood and it's easily moved from one place to another. And today, as I was vacuuming, I shifted the shelf with my shoulder and a lot of books fell onto the floor. Sanja came to help me put them back. And I remembered something: when he came by to see us the first day after we returned from the hospital, Asim used precisely that image to describe her state after the stroke. "It's as though an earthquake had knocked books off a shelf onto the parquet," he said. "And now each one has to be put back in its proper place."

It's been three months since her stroke, and her bosses haven't even telephoned to say hello and find out how she is, whether she's recovering. That's probably how it is everywhere in the world. So I arranged a meeting at her firm. In my telephone conversations and email exchanges, R. (an official in Human

Resources) kept giving me contradictory answers, so I had no confidence in her explanations about Sanja's rights and obligations. And, in a word, if I hadn't called her yesterday, I wouldn't have known that Sanja's employment comes to an end on the sixth of August. How come, since she hasn't yet used her holiday days? R. maintains that she hasn't yet received approval for that from her boss, who's on leave. That's why I've asked for this meeting, to try to get some concrete answers in writing. R. kept me waiting in the lobby, after a young man in uniform at the entrance to the Conference of Catholic Bishops of America instructed me fairly authoritatively to sit to one side and wait. After a while, R. appeared, led me into a conference room, and showed me where I was to sit, but she herself remained standing, near the door. She put down a sheet of paper with the explanations. I suggested that she sit down, as though I were at home here and she the visitor. And she said, no, no, she'd stand. This is an unusual situation: I'm sitting, reading, while she stands, rigid, at a distance. It's presumably not that she's afraid of my violent reactions, and so she's uncertain, staying on her feet, so that she can run away in the event that I charge angrily in her direction. I insist that she sits down, because she's making me nervous. She does so reluctantly, her shirt done up to the highest button, but she has pulled the pendant on the chain around her neck onto her collar: a gold German iron cross. "Are you German?" I ask. Out of a need to mollify her, I tell her that I work for German television. She looks at me fairly coldly and, instead of replying, points at the paper in front of me.

The moment I got home, I had to take a hot shower. "I've never experienced such coldness! I'm frozen right through!" I tell Sanja.

And she laughs and says: "What do you expect? It's the Vatican! A corporation that officially uses a dead language!"

Her isolation. When I get home from work I run up the stairs, and she opens the door as I reach it. Smiling. I thought that she watched from the window for the old Ford Taurus to appear in the parking lot, and then went to the door to open it before I rang the bell. But it isn't like that. She says she doesn't look out the window, but waits by the door, watching through the spy hole.

When I get home from work, we have coffee and remember the past. Every day. And I always hope she will have woken up that morning and recalled everything. In our conversations, we often go through the list of addresses where we've lived. She remembers some of the places, but not others. We lived in Zagreb for a few months, for instance, and she remembers that. She left Sarajevo with Harun in September 1995. The town was still besieged, a driver from the Soros Open Society Foundation drove them over the airport runway, to Konjic, where they got into a truck and that took them to Split. Two days passed before I could speak to them, by then they were already staying with my Zagreb acquaintances Nenad and Marija, whom Sanja had met then for the first time. In our short telephone conversation, she told me that she and Harun were fine, that the journey had been exhausting, and that they were resting. She said that Marija and Nenad were good people. I asked her: "How do you know?" And she replied: "Because in their house a cat and a dog live together."

She's finding her isolation increasingly hard. We decided to start learning Spanish in the hope that this would help fill her day with interesting content. As long as I've known her, she has praised the music of the Spanish language. "Just don't hurry me, you have your rhythm, and I have mine, I'll learn slowly. *Poco a poco!*" she says. In fact, she doubts that the two of us can study together. Once, thirty years ago, the differences between us were so great that it's a real miracle we're still together. Her recollection of the past century is more intensive than her memory of the twenty-first. She says: "We're a dog and a cat who've been living together for thirty years now." What's important for her is the accord that's rarely established between natural enemies. The rule is that cats and dogs don't like each other, and when it happens that they can, after all, put up with each other, that is a harmony that makes this world a better place. Over time, we've reached an accord. Or it would be more accurate to say that the differences between us are increasingly slight. We differ the way a Spanish r differs from a French one.

At 7:00 a.m., before I set off to work, I make her coffee; she prepares my lunch, goes back to bed, and sleeps for another hour. She drinks her coffee when it's cold. For the rest of the day, until I come home, she invents jobs for herself as a refuge from loneliness. For her forgetfulness, it's very important that everything is always left in the same place, so that she can find things more easily. But, to fill the time she spends alone, she moves objects around the apartment and rearranges the furniture. Today she sent me an email. Subject: Call me. And underneath, an explanation: *I don't know where I've left my phone.* I called her, she set off toward the source of the sound and so found her phone. Last year something similar happened, only the roles were reversed. She was in Sarajevo, I couldn't find my phone, so I sent her an email asking her to call me. And she did, and the sound came from the washing machine, where I'd put my jeans I had earlier spilled coffee on. She called in time, so the phone wasn't drowned in water and detergent. That's so simple: she phoned me from a different continent to save me from my forgetfulness. It's a shame there isn't a machine that discovers forgotten events and returns them to the memory.

✦

On my way to work, a text message from her arrived on my phone: "Do you remember when we were children, little girls wore crocheted collars on their school smocks..." It was early in the morning, and she was in the depths of her childhood.

Two hours later she called to say: "I've ironed all your T-shirts, and I kissed every one."

And here I am, I can't stop thinking about those kisses, as though a hundred cats were tickling my soul with their soft paws.

We had put on our best clothes. I was driving south along the wide Route 66, when the car began to slow down. I pressed the accelerator, but the vehicle had trouble gaining speed. Then we slowed to a standstill, stopping on the hard shoulder. We got out of the Taurus and looked at gray smoke curling up from it. I had the feeling that at any minute the smoke would turn into fire and the car into an inferno. And the more I touched the Taurus, the dirtier I became. Irritated, I made an effort not to convey my irritation to Sanja. She had tamed the wind in her hair by pushing her sunglasses onto the top of her head; her gold necklace gleamed in the sun. She was young again! I touched her face with my filthy hand, and she wiped the soot from my brow, straightening my eyebrows. The smell of spit and memories of childhood. We were already late for where we had headed, but my irritation had completely disappeared, we laughed, hugging, without really knowing where our happiness had come from. And then a pigeon landed right beside our car. This isn't exactly a place where you expect such a bird to appear. You won't find any seeds to peck here, my dear! It waddled about fearlessly, wound itself around our shoes . . . An unusual pigeon, its legs were covered in feathers right down to its claws. A feather-shanked pigeon. *Golub gaćan*, I say, that's what it was called in our childhood.

Holding hands, we step into the circular glass door through which I have often passed over the last months. Our moving shadows break up in the glass. The melancholy of late summer. We go up in the elevator to the fourth floor. We're in the hospital for a routine medical examination. We sit and wait. In the silence, we look at a painting in front of us by an anonymous artist. And then Sanja asks: "Isn't it a pitiful destiny for an artist for their works to end up on the wall of a doctor's waiting room . . . ?"

Toward midnight, in the apartment above us, someone is moving furniture and the feet of tables scrape over the floor. I don't know why this is repeated every night. Once, when the noise was insupportable, I went upstairs and banged on the door, which no one opened. I don't know who lives in the apartment above ours. I don't know why they drag their furniture over the floor on top of our heads just before midnight. But I'd like to know. That restlessness of the tenant above us doesn't last long, not more than two or three minutes, and after that I always become aware of the silence that surrounds us.

Today, in a book, I found the following description: It's 1913, and the setting is the Grand Hôtel de Cabourg. Marcel Proust has rented five rooms, one for him to stay in and the other four so that there is silence.

She says: "It's the twenty-first century now, but I had a friend who was born in the nineteenth."

We often refer to years, and we've become quite childish already. I feel pretty tranquil. It's enough for her to straighten the collar of my shirt, and that touch calms everything in the universe. Misfortune has reduced us to our essence. And nothing is left of us, apart from love.

Today we went to Tony's Auto, at our old Alexandria address, where we've had all our cars fixed over the last twenty years. Repairs to the Taurus would cost nearly three thousand dollars, and that's more than the vehicle is worth. We gave up the old Ford, and the one-eyed mechanic said they could quote for it to be taken to the car cemetery. I took my personal belongings from the glovebox in front of the passenger seat, mostly documents, pens, and loose change, and we bade the Taurus farewell. I didn't feel particularly sad.

When we turned from there into Fayette Street, we stopped to let a car with a camera on the roof and the inscription GOOGLE on its door go past, they were filming the street for that Street View on their map. Just here, in the building behind us, was where we had lived until five years ago, and then we moved, fleeing from painful memories. After today's chance filming, I thought about our being imprisoned for a long time at our old address. On the film we would have blurred faces, so that no one would be able to recognize us and so our privacy would be protected. For a moment I was pleased about all that, but then, once I had become aware of it, my pleasure was transformed into apprehension.

We'd left our green umbrella in the trunk of the Taurus, but we didn't feel like going back.

SEMEZDIN MEHMEDINOVIĆ
is a Bosnian writer. When the Bosnian War
broke out in 1992, Mehmedinović published an
early version of *Sarajevo Blues* and, with a group
of friends, founded the weekly political magazine *BH Dani* (*Days*), a voice for democracy and
pluralism in times of genocide. In 1996, after
the end of the Siege of Sarajevo, Mehmedinović
emigrated to the United States with his family
and lived in the D.C. area for more than twenty
years. He now lives in Sarajevo.

CELIA HAWKESWORTH has translated nearly forty books from the Serbo-Croatian, by authors including Ivo Andrić, Dubravka Ugrešić, and Daša Drndić. Her translation of Ivo Andrić's *Omer Pasha Latas* won the Oxford-Weidenfeld Prize in 2019, and her translation of Daša Drndić's *EEG* won the Best Translated Book Award in 2020. She lives in Oxfordshire, England.